The Wanderer's Guide To Dragon Keeping

Ashley O'Melia

ashleyomelia.com

Book Layout © 2014 BookDesignTemplates.com
Cover art by Artistic Photography by Sydney, photosbysydney.com

The Wanderer's Guide to Dragon Keeping/Ashley O'Melia. -- 1st ed.
ISBN 978-1495406515

Dedicated to Jay, who is at least mostly responsible for my love of fantasy.

CONTENTS

Prologue

"Aubrey! It's time to come down for lunch!"

The little girl sighed as she heard her mother's voice drift up the stairs to her. She regretfully stepped down from the window seat, where she had been the damsel in distress for the past twenty minutes. Even though her Ken doll had not come to save her yet, she wasn't really ready to stop. She picked her way to the door. The dress-up trunk had spewed dresses, scarves, tiaras, and costume jewelry onto the floor, amongst books and toys. "Coming, Mama," she replied, but probably not loud enough for her mother to hear.

She slunk down the stairs and to the kitchen. The smell of her mother's homemade soup met her halfway down the staircase, and promised plenty of bread to go with it. The honey butter would be even better.

"Honey, why are you still wearing your princess dress?" her mother asked as she entered the room. "You know we're going to leave right after lunch to go shopping."

"I know," Aubrey replied as she sat down at the table. "I just didn't want to stop playing. The dragon hadn't even had a chance to lock the castle door yet." She looked down at her lap, admiring the pink satin as it draped itself around the chair.

"You will have plenty of time when we get back. And maybe you could use some of your birthday money to buy a new book? Or whatever else we might find. It's been awhile since we've gone downtown, and it's not like we're just going for a boring old grocery trip. You should be excited." Her mother placed a bowl of soup in front of her, along with two fat buttered rolls. "Just be sure you hurry up and change after lunch, okay?"

"Oh, thank you, Mama! I sure will!" She dug hastily into the fresh rolls.

The sound of crunching gravel drifted in through the open kitchen window, and her mother turned from the stove to look out the door. "It's your dad," she said.

"Daddy!" Aubrey was out of her seat and out the door before her mother could reprimand her to sit down and eat. She raced to her father as he climbed out of his sedan. "What are you doing home?"

Her father wrapped his arms around her, princess dress and all, and carried her towards the house. "Well, hello to you, too! I had things fairly well wrapped up at the office, and I thought I would take off so I could come shopping with you two!"

"Really, Jim?" Her mother asked from the open doorway. "That would be wonderful! I can't remember the last time you were off work for anything fun."

"Daddy, will you take us to the toystore?" Aubrey asked.

Her father set her back down in front of her soup. "Katie says there's a whole new display of nothing but magic tricks and I really want to see it!"

He smiled at her over the steaming bowl of soup Mama had just set down in front of him. "I'm sure we could do that. You think you could be the next great magician?"

"Just watch my lunch magically disappear!" she announced as she slurped her soup.

"You really do have to change clothes, Aubrey," her mother announced when she had finished. The satisfied smile that the buttered rolls had brought to Aubrey's face quickly faded to a small frown.

"Oh, just let her wear it," her father said. "It'd be fun to go shopping with a princess."

"The dragon is going to get you, Mama!" Aubrey cried from the backseat. She made the little plastic dragon in her hand stomp around the headrest of her mother's seat.

"No, no! Not a dragon in my hair!" Mama waved her arms and shook her head. "I need a knight in shining armor!"

Her father plucked a silver pen out of the cup holder. "I'll save you!" He poked at the dragon with the pen. "Feel the wrath of my sword, dragon!"

Aubrey giggled as her dragon flew back to his place next to her in the backseat. "He might not be so easy to defeat next time, Daddy! He might breathe fire! Or, or learn magic. Yeah! Dragon magic!"

"Did you hear that, honey?" her father asked. "That's going to be one powerful little dragon."

"Sounds like I might have to get myself a helmet," her mother replied. "Oh, there's the turn for the mall."

Her father smoothly piloted the car off the highway and around the ramp. Aubrey watched intently out the window as the mall came into view. Not exactly a castle, but exciting nonetheless. "Can I bring my dragon in with me?"

"Does it fit in your purse?" Daddy asked.

She opened her sequined purse and pushed the dragon down inside next to her lip gloss and her mother's old wallet that she had given Aubrey to use. The sides of the purse bulged a little bit, but it worked. "Yep! I'm ready to go!"

Even though the mall hadn't changed much since their last trip, Aubrey was fascinated by everything there was to see. The crowd pressed around her as she studied the bright signs over each of the stores. The escalators stretched away from her like giant undulating snakes. Huge fountains spurted water into glittering arcs.

"I'm going to make a wish!" she exclaimed. Detaching herself from her mother's hand, she dug in her purse for some pennies. The little plastic dragon stared up at her from the satin-lined depths. "Mama, I found a nickel. Do you think I would get five wishes if I used it?"

But as she looked up to her mother for the answer, Aubrey heard a sound so loud that it drowned out all other noises in the mall. Flame and bits of merchandise exploded into the air from a kiosk only a few yards away from them. Mama turned away from the fiasco and threw herself on top of Aubrey, just as the second explosion sounded.

Aubrey heard the whoosh of water around her as they crashed headlong into the fountain. Somehow she managed to free her arms from her mother's strong grasp as they fell, and caught herself before her head hit the bottom of the shallow pool.

"Mama! Mama, what's going on?" She shook her mother's arm, but she didn't answer. Blood trickled from the back of Mama's head, down her cheek and into the water. Her eyes were open in a look of surprised terror, but she didn't blink as Aubrey squirmed out from underneath her.

She had lost her purse, but the little plastic dragon floated just a few feet away and she scooped him up. Aubrey stood up in the fountain. The crowd was swiftly dispersing, clamoring to get away from the fiery kiosk. She searched desperately for her father, but she couldn't see him. "Daddy?" She stood there, the bloody water up to her knees, watching the last few people stream toward the exit, clutching the little dragon to her chest. She stood there for what seemed like hours, as the water ran off her dress and into the fountain, and turned pink around her and her mother's body.

She was knocked out of her stupor when a security guard swooped her out of the fountain and carried her out of the mall.

The rest of the day was a blur. People had asked her questions, looked her over, and asked more questions, but she answered without knowing what she said. She knew there was a hospital involved, and maybe a police station before she was delivered to the steps of a large dismal house downtown that said 'Littlewood Foster Home for Girls' over the door.

A heavyset woman with a lined but not unkind face, who said she was Ms. Clavens, led her up the stairs and down a dim hallway. The bedroom she left her in was clean but barren, with only a few beds and dressers.

"What about my dress-up trunk?" Aubrey asked, speaking

voluntarily for the first time since the incident. "And my books?"

"You can't have all of that here. Supper is in an hour."

Aubrey set her dragon down on the bed that the woman had said was hers. She ran a finger disdainfully over the scratchy blanket, but pulled it away from the pillow and climbed in. She lay next to her dragon, in a foster home, in her ruined princess dress.

Time at the orphanage was indeterminate. The daily routine was the same whether it was Sunday or Wednesday. The girls rose promptly out of bed at 6:30 for breakfast, and were sent off for their chores as soon as they set their spoons down. This quickly brought them to lunch, then studies, then baths and bedtime. There were no bedtime stories, only a headcount before the lights went out.

And so it was that Aubrey had no idea how long she had been there when Ms. Clavens summoned her to the office. As she crept up to the cracked office door, she could hear Ms. Clavens talking to someone.

"Well I just can't tell you how thrilled I am that you decided to come to me to find the newest member of your family. So many times the adoption agencies manage to overlook us, and we are positively full to the brim." Ms. Clavens gave a little laugh almost like a giggle, which Aubrey had never heard come out of her before. "Now, then. I think I may have just the girl for you. You said you wanted just one child, correct?"

"Yes, ma'am," came a scratchy voice.

"Alright then. You'll forgive me for double-checking, it's

just that I do have a couple sets of sisters that I'd really rather not split up, and seeing as how you don't have any children of your own I thought it might be a decent fit for you."

"Our home is really only suited for us to have one child."

"Yes, of course. Well, you'll like our little Aubrey. She's quite shy, but I think she's still in a bit of shock after the death of her parents, poor thing. You remember those terrorists blowing up the mall last month? Her parents were two of the victims. They found the poor girl standing in a fountain next to her dead mother! Can you believe it? I'm glad to say she is the only orphan that we saw from that accident, thank goodness. Plenty of our girls go through quite a bit of tragedy before they end up on my doorstep."

"And there weren't any other family members to take her?" asked a woman's voice.

"The only relative the police were able to find was an aunt in Oregon, but she had health issues and said she wouldn't be able to keep her."

Aubrey put up a shaking hand to knock on the door.

"Come in, dear!" called Ms. Clavens. "Aubrey this is Mr. and Mrs. Goodknight."

One

Aubrey fiddled with the edge of her paper gown as she took in the bland surroundings of the exam room. The walls were painted a pale, sickly blue that only intensified the bleak whiteness of the ceiling and floor. Even the paper gown was a dreary grey.

She never imagined that she would be here for this. She had been healthy. Even as a kid, she was usually the last one in the class to get the flu. She couldn't remember the last time she had the flu since school, as a matter of fact. Aubrey hadn't even been to the doctor for a regular exam in years. There didn't seem to be any need for it. At least, there hadn't been until a couple weeks ago.

Aubrey had been getting ready for work when she found the lump. At first she thought it was just her underwire causing some irritation, but when she reached under her bra to fix it her fingers found the lump instead. She tried not to panic. *People get lumps all the time right? It doesn't necessarily* mean *anything.* *It doesn't* have *to be cancerous.* She was able to get an appointment that afternoon, and her doctor was quick to schedule a biopsy.

There was a gentle knock on the door, and Dr. Crawford entered the room accompanied by a nurse in purple scrubs. Aubrey looked to the doctor expectantly. He had her file in his hand and seemed to be studying it in great detail.

"Well the results of the biopsy are positive," he said matter-of-factly without looking up at her. "What this means is that we need to schedule a full body scan. Now, don't panic. I don't expect that anything has metastasized to other regions yet even though the cancer is in a relatively advanced stage. But we want to be safe about things, and know exactly what we're dealing with before we proceed." Dr. Crawford finally looked up from the file to gauge Aubrey's reaction. The nurse gazed at her sympathetically.

Aubrey couldn't help but feel stricken. She had known there was a chance the test would be positive, but she had been trying to put it out of her mind so much that she hadn't thought about what she would do if it was. Her heart beat loudly enough she was sure she wasn't the only one who could hear it. She looked at the doctor with his furrowed brow, at the nurse with her purple scrubs, and at the outdated wallpaper border. "Okay. So what do we do after the scan?"

Dr. Crawford nodded and buried his nose in the file once again. "It looks as though the tumor will be operable, so we will need to schedule you for surgery. Provided we're able to get it all, you may not have to undergo chemotherapy, but we won't really know until we get in there. Of course, all of that will depend on what we do or don't find on the body scan. You can see Lucy at the front desk to get the scan scheduled, and she will also talk to you about your financial options. We'll go from there. Nurse?" Dr. Crawford waved the file vaguely in the nurse's direction, then turned and left the room.

The nurse stepped up to where Aubrey sat on the exam table and handed her a fistful of brochures and pamphlets. "These will explain all of the procedures for you. Some of the information doesn't directly apply to your case but I still suggest reading through it. Do you have anyone close to you that is going to be helping you get through this?"

Aubrey stared down at the bundle of paperwork for a moment before she slowly reached up and relieved the nurse of it. She thought about her adoptive parents. The only time she talked with them was when she went to visit them at the cemetery. She had no brothers or sisters. Her parents hadn't been from here, so there was no extended family around. This all seemed suddenly much more forlorn than she had ever thought it to be. "I have a few friends," she told the nurse lamely.

"Well there's also a flyer for a support group in here." The nurse gently pulled a bright yellow piece of paper out from the bottom of the stack in Aubrey's hand and placed it on top. "I've sent a lot of patients to that group and they say it really helps. It makes a big difference to talk to someone who has actually been through it. They meet on Monday nights at the community center. We'll see you after your scan!" The nurse and her purple scrubs whisked out of the room, leaving Aubrey in her paper gown with a handful of brochures.

Aubrey had taken the entire day off work for her doctor's appointment. She hadn't really wanted to let anybody at work know what was going on, but of course her boss had to pry when she asked for some time off.

"It's not really going to take all day, though, right? Couldn't you come back to work afterwards?"

"No, I'd like to think I won't be there that long, Mr. Milner," Aubrey had relented. "But I've got some things going on and I don't think I will really be of a mindset to work once I'm done. I really just need the whole day."

Her boss had glowered at her over his wireframes from behind his desk. He was a stickler for punctuality and attendance. She couldn't think of a time he had ever not been at the office. She had even once come in on a Saturday when she had forgotten something, and ran into Mr. Milner sans toupee. They were both startled, enough so that she couldn't remember what she had come there for in the first place.

"That's fine, I guess. But make sure you have the monthly report done the day before so we won't have to wait on it. We have a lot going on here, too."

Having secured her day off, Aubrey decided to spend the rest of it on herself. She headed down to the library. Story Hour would be starting soon, and she normally couldn't catch the ones during the weekdays for preschoolers. It would be nice to be there for a different crowd than the usual.

The kids' section of the library always fascinated her. It was really quite large, to begin with, nothing like the small corner of an old damp building in the town they lived in when she was small. If the amazing selection of books wasn't enough, there were beanbag chairs, couches, rugs for kids to relax on, and a huge papier mache dragon hung from the ceiling. Talk about atmosphere. Children were thrilled to be at the library, and Aubrey often heard the plaintive wail of a small child being dragged out the front doors by her mother, not wanting to leave this wonderful place.

"Well, Aubrey! What are you doing here, dear?" asked Emma, the elderly librarian. "I didn't expect to see you until Saturday."

"I ended up with a day off, and I thought I would come and see if you needed any help with Story Hour."

"Oh, how delightful!" Emma replied in an almost-too-loud-for-the-library voice. "As a matter of fact, I really could use your help. Stacey is at home with strep throat, poor thing, so I was going to have to do the story myself. I don't mind but I do hate to leave the circulation desk. Although I'm sure I would be too distracted with the kiddies to bother coming back to it." Emma laughed.

"No problem," said Aubrey. "What book would you like me to read?" Small children were starting to filter in, and gathered around the rocking chair in the corner of the kids' section. They held their mother's hands tightly as they came in from the street, but let go and bolted for the rugs and beanbags as soon as they saw them.

"Oh, this one here." Emma reached under her desk and handed a hardcover picture book to Aubrey. The cover was a picture of a little boy riding a dragon. "A lovely little fantasy story for them today."

Aubrey couldn't help but smile. Maybe a lovely little fantasy story was just what she needed, too. Anything to help her forget about what was actually going on inside her body right now. She took the book and headed for the rocking chair, glancing at the dragon above her head as she went. She thought about how life used to be for her, what seemed like a very long time ago, a time when she used to believe in magic, and dragons, and if she had thought about it maybe even a world where cancer didn't exist. She would read any fantasy book she could get her hands on, and spent hours and hours escaping into other lives and other worlds.

Everything had changed after the incident at the mall. There was no longer room in her life for fantasy and magic, only hard reality. *Maybe it's time to start dreaming a little more*, she thought as she studied the book's cover.

She settled herself into the rocking chair and looked at the expectant faces that surrounded her. *Such sweet innocence.* She read the book, holding it out to show each picture and making sure every child could see. They didn't say much as the story introduced a little boy named Richard, but they oohed and aahed as Richard flew on his pet dragon. Their parents tried to calm them, but it was really quite useless and nobody truly minded the small disturbance.

When the story was through, some of the kids came up to Aubrey to look at the pictures again or to get hugs. She always loved this part of helping out at the library. The kids never treated her like a stranger. One little boy had been staring at the cover of the book for quite some time.

"Did you enjoy the story?" asked Aubrey.

The little boy studied the book for a couple seconds more. "Yeah, but I would like it better if it was real."

"Oh, I see," she chuckled. "Wanting your own dragon to fly around on, huh?"

He nodded. "I think I'll ask for one for my birthday."

"That might be kind of hard for someone to come by."

The little boy looked up from his book and shot his blue gaze right into Aubrey's eyes. "But wouldn't it be the most magical thing if dragons were real?"

Aubrey thought about the little plastic dragon that reigned

over a dusty corner of her bookshelf at home. "It certainly would."

Two

When the children had checked out their books and left the library, Aubrey decided to look for one herself. It had been awhile since she had found time for a good read. She wandered through the stacks, trailing her fingers across the spines of the books. She inhaled deeply. The musty papery smell was even better than the smell of coffee.

She thought a lot about what the little boy had said. She wished books came alive for her the way they did for children, the way they used to. Maybe she needed that sort of escape, too. She browsed through the romance books, but they weren't really her cup of tea. *Silly, simpering women being courted by roguish devils who finally realized the error of their ways. No thanks.* She skimmed over the historical fiction. She liked this genre, but there would be too many characters dying, and that was the last thing she needed right now. She never cared for nonfiction much at all, so she skipped right over that. There was enough nonfiction in real life.

She at last found herself at the end of a stack surrounded by fantasy novels, the grown-up versions of what she had enjoyed so much when she was little. She hoped that dragons stayed real for that little boy.

Glancing through the authors and titles, she squatted down to look at the bottom shelf and her eyes landed on an old dusty volume. Its leather cover was cracked and worn around the edges, and the pages had yellowed. The spine didn't sport the usual white library sticker that indicated its spot on the shelves. Aubrey pulled the book out from between its neighbors. She expected to find a title on the front cover, but there wasn't one. Curious, she opened the book. *The Wanderer's Guide to Dragon Keeping* crawled across the title page in an odd script. Flipping through the book, she found the typeset to be oddly whimsical. She took it to the circulation desk.

"Did you find what you needed, dear?" asked Emma.

"Well, I'm really not sure to be honest. I found this book, but it's not labeled. There isn't even the stamp with the library's name on the inside of the cover."

Emma took the book from Aubrey's hands and looked it over. "I guess it must have been in the book sale and gotten misplaced. I'd say it belongs to you now." She looked up at Aubrey and smiled as she handed the book back. "It certainly looks like it will be an interesting read for you."

Mystified, Aubrey took the book and headed for the door. It was such a strange thing, but she wasn't one to turn down a free book. She got in her car and put the book on the seat next to her.

Back at home, she started to make dinner. She sautéed

free-range chicken tenders in olive oil, sliced a tomato from the farmer's market, and microwaved an organic potato. Not quite the pizza and soda she consumed in her college days, she had changed her diet considerably in the short time since she had found out about the tumor. There was bountiful information flooding the internet on anti-cancer diets, and while she wasn't willing to survive solely on fennel seeds she didn't think it could hurt to get a little healthier.

She poured herself a glass of double-filtered water, and took her meal to the breakfast nook. Staring out the kitchen window as she nibbled on the chicken, her mind wandered back to the book. Aubrey couldn't quite get over how strange it all was. Thoughts of the book gave her a quivering feeling of excitement in her stomach that she hadn't felt in a long time. She abandoned her dinner and retrieved the book from the seat of her car. She handled the book carefully. Even though it was free, she didn't want the leather binding to crack any more than it already had. She skimmed through the table of contents.

Introduction – Read First

I. Hatching Your Dragonette
II. Bathing and Grooming
III. Your Dragonette's First Feeding
IV. Draconian Knowledge of Humans
V. Fire and Flying
VI. Interaction with Non-Wanderers
VII. A Warning to Wanderers
VIII. Guiding Your Dragon Home

Well, she had certainly wanted some fantasy reading, and here it was. She decided to heed the directions and read the introduction first.

Introduction – Read First

Welcome to <u>The Wanderer's Guide to Dragon Keeping</u>. You no doubt have stumbled upon this book due to a great need, whether realized or otherwise. You are a very select individual, placed in a very exclusive position of responsibility. Dragon keeping is not for the faint of heart.

While we are sure that you understand the importance of your position, it is imperative that you do not read ahead. *You may be tempted to do this with the idea of learning more about your charge, but we promise it will only hinder the growth and development of both Wanderer and Dragonette. Do not proceed from here to Chapter I until the time is right.*

Then, written in a large, loopy hand,

Good luck.

Aubrey flipped back to the title page to look for the author. She needed to find out what humor writer this was, because this seemed like it was going to be good. The title page, though, contained only the title. She checked the spine of the book, the inside of both the front and back covers, and even punched in the title online. No luck.

With a sigh, she once again obeyed the book's orders and did not proceed to the first chapter. The only thing this time was right for, was curling up and going to bed. There had been too much going on today and she could feel her energy draining out of her like sand.

Three

The keys clicked like a possessed metronome, hypnotizing Aubrey as she worked up the monthly reports. She threw herself into every number, reveling in the concrete calculation on the spreadsheet. This was real. This was constant. This never changed or did things unexpected, and if it did she could fix the problem with a few clicks.

"Hey."

Click click click.

"Hey."

Click click click.

"Aubrey!"

Aubrey looked up with a start to find Betty's face peering down at her over the cubicle wall. "Oh, hey. Sorry. I was kind of involved. What's up?"

"I didn't think I'd ever tear you away from your monitors! I wish I had the dedication that you do. Or maybe I don't. I'm not sure that would suit me. Anyway, are you ready to hit the carnival tonight?" Betty's fifties coif and horn-rimmed glassed perfectly suited her heart-shaped face and curvy figure, adorned today in a vintage black and white polka dot dress. Aubrey twinged inside at her own drab sweater and dress slacks.

Aubrey tipped back in her office chair and sighed. "I'm not sure, Betty," she replied. "I had a doctor's appointment yesterday, and I'm still kind of worn out from it."

"Uh oh." Betty's face disappeared from the top of the wall and rematerialized around the edge of it, this time with her body attached. "Sounds bad. I should have asked you about that first. Spill it, girl."

"I don't really want the whole office talking about this."

"You know I'm not going to tell anybody. Things do have a way of getting around this place though, you know? Might as well start the rumor with the truth."

Aubrey snorted as she thought about Angela from accounting's divorce. She hadn't been married long, but the entire office building knew that the paperwork had been filed even before her husband did. That certainly wasn't Betty's fault though. She heaved another sigh and avoided looking Betty in the eyes. "It's cancer."

"Oh, honey, I am so sorry." Betty laid a sympathetic arm around Aubrey's shoulder. Aubrey tried to focus on the new tattoo poking out from beneath the sleeve of Betty's dress to keep the tears in her eyes from spilling over. "What's the plan?"

"They're going to do a body scan to see if it's anywhere else before I go under the knife for it. Any kind of treatment after the surgery is just up in the air, from what I can tell. It's just a waiting game right now, and it's driving me crazy."

"Is there anything I can do? Do you need me to go with you to the scan?"

Aubrey shook her head. "Thank you, but I don't think there is. It would be wonderful to have you there with me, but then we would both have to take off work. I'm going to have to ask for time off for the scan and then for surgery. I'm hoping Mr. Milner doesn't ask too many questions."

Betty perched on the corner of the desk and frowned. "Even just you taking off work and having surgery is going to get around like wildfire. I promise I won't tell, but I can't promise nobody else will. And at least think about the carnival, okay? It will help take your mind off things."

Later that day, Aubrey plopped down in the break room while she waited for her frozen organic meal to finish cooking in the microwave. She rummaged around in her purse for the zip lock baggie of all-natural sunflower seeds she had packed, but her hand came in contact with the book instead. She had thrown it in there this morning with the idea of reading on her break, but she didn't really know if it was the right time to read it yet. *Stupid girl,* she thought, *obeying a fictional book.*

Even so, she held the book against the edge of the table and considered the cover again. *How could there be no author? Wouldn't they want the credit for this?* For the first time she noticed tiny holes in the corner of the cover, like minute teeth marks.

"What are you reading?" came a voice from over her shoulder. Startled, Aubrey dropped the book, and it landed open to the title page. She bent over to pick it up but Ben was faster. "*The Wanderer's Guide to Dragon Keeping*? Sounds like my kind of thing. I didn't know you were into fantasy books."

For what seemed like the millionth time that day, Aubrey sighed. Ben had been trying to strike up a conversation ever since he started with the company a couple weeks ago. Aubrey had been trying just as hard to avoid him. He worked in the IT department and seemed nice enough, but sparking a work relationship just did not seem the right thing to do.

"I think the newbie likes you," Betty had whispered conspiratorially after Ben had introduced himself for the first time. They had been right here, in the break room, and Ben had broken off a conversation about string theory with one of the other computer guys to say hi to her.

"No, he doesn't. He's just being nice," she had whispered back. "And I don't think he's my type, anyway." Aubrey had looked him over a little more as he had returned to his table. Not bad, but super nerdy. *Probably spends all weekend playing Halo.*

"And just what exactly is your type? I haven't seen you with a guy in how long?"

"Touché. But it isn't that."

"Oh, come on," Betty had teased. "Get your nerd on!"

Now, Aubrey looked him over again, but watching him examine the book drained any potential passion from her body. "It's just something I came across at the library. It seemed interesting. Can I have it back please?" she asked nervously.

Ben carefully turned the book over in his hands. "It looks like it's quite old. Do you know anything about it?" He frowned as he scrutinized the lack of information on the title page.

"No, not really." She continued to hold her hand out for

the book.

"I have a friend that specializes in antique books. He moonlights buying and selling them online. I can take it to him and see what he has to say about it if you like."

Aubrey felt her heart leap up in her throat a bit at the thought of letting such an old book into anyone else's hands. It was bad enough being in Ben's. "Oh, no, I appreciate it but I really shouldn't have even let it out of the house."

Ben nodded his agreement. "Well if you want to we could take it to him together, if you're interested."

"Maybe some other time."

"Okay," Ben shrugged. He started to turn back toward the break room door, but he paused midstride and turned back to look at her. "Hey, Aubrey? There are a bunch of people getting together at the park this weekend for LARP, if you'd like to come."

"LARP?"

"Live Action Role Play. Everyone gets dressed up in fantasy costumes and has a little fun. You know, knights, dragons, mythical creatures."

"Um…." Aubrey felt a familiar panic rising in her, just like any other time she wanted to say no to someone. *Do grown people really do this?*

"It's okay, nevermind. I just thought you might enjoy it. I know it seems a little silly, but it's as close to the fantasy in that book as you are going to get." Ben turned back toward the door.

"Wait!" said Audrey's mouth before her mind had a moment to argue. "What character do you play?"

Ben smiled. "King Arthur, of course." He disappeared through the break room door.

Four

The black figure crept around the corner of the building, avoiding the security lights. He had been casing the place for awhile now. It wasn't the kind of place that would normally expect a burglar, so it didn't merit the usual security system. A couple of lights and a steel door were all that stood between him and his goal.

He had been in the building during business hours that day, and had unlocked a window on the first floor as he casually looked around. Not wanting to gamble on whether or not they checked the windows at night, he had brought his glass cutter just in case.

He didn't need it. The window slid open with barely a noise, and he climbed in. It was darker than he had expected in here. He flicked on his flashlight and started looking through the rows of books. Perhaps he should have taken the book when he was there earlier, but there were too many people around. The old lady at the desk had a good eye, he could tell, and he wasn't about to raise her suspicion by trying to sneak the book out.

"You're too late." He dropped the flashlight as he spun around toward the voice. It rolled to a stop against the speaker's orthopedic shoes, shining underneath the stacks and making eerie geometric shadows of the books. "She already has it. It wouldn't do you any good, anyway. Shall I call your boss and let him know you're here? I doubt you have his approval."

The boss didn't want him to take the book in the first place. When he had suggested it, the withering glare that his boss shot him should have told him to keep his ideas to himself, but Leonard was not convinced. If the Wanderer didn't have the book, she wouldn't know what to do at all. Surely that would be better for them. And maybe it would even get him a promotion.

Well, not now.

"I suggest you make your way out of here before I do something I haven't had to do in a very long time."

Leonard sprinted back to the open window and leapt out.

Five

The lights and sounds of the carnival were a time machine for Aubrey. The glare and hoopla called up those hot summer nights when her small hometown would turn the park into a grand fair, with food, rides, and vendors. On those nights, she could have been anyone other than Aubrey Goodknight. The humid air would wrap itself around her and make her part of the carnival, far more than just a paying guest. It was like a whole other world for a little while. She once made the mistake of driving by just as the fair was leaving town. Bits of trash blew across the grass and got hung up in the trees. The trucks and trailers that the carneys drove to the next town's fair seemed too normal and everyday with their faded logos and balding tires. It was as though, along with the rides and the tents and the lights, they had packed up the magic.

She tried not to think about that tonight, though.

"You want the rest of my funnel cake?" asked Betty.

"No, thanks. I'm full," Aubrey replied as she took the last

bite of her deep-fried Twinkie.

"You girls are so bad!" cried Angela from accounting. Betty had invited several of the girls from the office to go with them. "I can't even imagine how many calories are in those horrible things!"

"Obviously, you have never tried one," said Kay, Mr. Milner's secretary. "If you had, you wouldn't care about the calories. They are too delicious for me to bother thinking about it!"

The other girls nodded their agreement, and Angela sulked. "I'm not the only one! You can't tell me that none of you care about your weight or your diet. Heck, I've seen Aubrey in the break room with her fruits and veggies and baked chicken. Nobody does that just for fun!"

The girls turned to look at Aubrey, waiting for her explanation. Not that she really should have had to explain anything. She shrugged as her cheeks burned. "It's not about the calories. I'm just trying to eat healthy, and stay away from processed foods, you know? Gotta spoil myself a little bit, though." Everyone seemed to accept that, and they walked on to the arts and crafts booths.

"You okay?" whispered Betty.

"Yeah, mostly."

"Soooo, Aubrey," Kay butted in. "I saw Ben talking to you in the break room today. Is there something I need to know?"

Aubrey could feel her face flushing again in the cool evening air. "No, Kay. There's nothing going on."

"Can't say I blame you. He seems like a weirdo," Angela remarked as she flipped her long blonde hair over her shoulder.

"Um, why do you say that?" Suddenly Aubrey was feeling even more nervous about her encounter with Ben today.

But Angela was too distracted by the booth they had come upon to answer. The tables at the front were covered in worn black velvet, and adorned with an array of trinkets. There were any number of vendors like this at fairs, but Aubrey couldn't help but look at what each one had to offer. Most of the girls flocked toward the jewelry, but Aubrey's eye landed on a beautiful little box. It was made of stone, and had a complex flower pattern etched into the lid. She picked it up to check the price: five dollars. Perfect.

"What'd you find?" asked Betty, setting down a bad reproduction necklace.

"Just this. I thought it would look nice on my dresser with some other little boxes I have. What do you think?"

"Um, don't look right now, but what I think is that the old man back there is watching you very intently."

Aubrey put the box down and pretended to peruse the other baubles, trying to get a glimpse at the man behind the table. He was, indeed, staring, and not at their entire group but directly at her. His rheumy eyes watched her over a long gray beard that covered his face and spilled down to his lap. She didn't think people wore beards like that anymore.

"I think you're right. Creepy," she whispered back. "It's not like I'm going to steal it or anything."

Her coworker nodded. "Let's get on to the next booth."

"Well, wait a second." Aubrey really liked that little box, and wasn't going to let the treasure of the evening slip through her hands just because of some old coot with a case of the stares. It was just a cheap little knick-knack, but she liked it. *It's the kind of thing I would regret not getting.*

She picked the box back up and handed it to the young girl behind the table. As she pulled her cash out of her pocket, she noticed the old man struggling with his cane to get up out of his chair.

"No, no, no. Wrong box," he muttered, his hoarse voice barely above a whisper. The young girl still had the box Aubrey wanted, but she moved back toward the old man to help him out of the chair. "Wait," he said. Aubrey could barely tell that the voice came from him, other than the fluttering of his beard. Obediently, she stayed firmly rooted.

The old man shuffled to the van parked next to the booth and opened the back door. He rummaged around a bit, long enough to make Aubrey start to feel antsy. *What is this crazy old geezer up to?* He eventually pulled out a large wooden trunk, and she was surprised he had the strength in his frail body to lift it. The girl behind the table made no move to help him, but just stood there with the flower box in her hand. Perhaps she knew better.

He opened the trunk and rummaged around some more inside of it, his beard flapping with inaudible mumblings. He paused, stood back up slowly, and turned to Aubrey with a wooden box.

This box was quite a bit larger than the stone one she had been trying to purchase. The old man had to use both of his shaky hands to hold it. The lid was an intricate design of different inlaid woods, spiraling in from the outer edges. Aubrey was nearly hypnotized by the swirling pattern.

"Um, how much?" she asked the old man, not sure what else to say.

He waived his hand dismissively. "It's yours," his beard wiggled. "No charge."

Aubrey stared at the box as the old man pushed it quietly into her hands. The craftsmanship was highly detailed. The smooth finish was almost waxy, instead of glossy. She gaped at the old man, speechless. She thought she may have seen a smile behind the beard.

He bent down to look under the table and came back up with a bag. He took the wooden box gently back from Aubrey and placed it in the bag. Tissue paper seemed to magically appear from underneath the table as well, and he took the stone box back from the young girl and wrapped it thoroughly. He placed it in the bag on top of the wooden box, and handed the bag to Aubrey.

Taking the handles of the bag, Aubrey looked at the young girl for confirmation. She didn't say a word. "Um, well, thank you." The old man flapped a wrinkly hand at her and hobbled back to his seat. Aubrey turned to catch up with her friends as they filtered away from the booth and on down the midway.

"Well that was certainly interesting," said Betty when they were out of earshot of the generous old man. "I'm used to people at carnivals trying to get as much money out of you as possible, not giving things away."

"My five-dollar funnel cake agrees with you," retorted Kay. "You didn't know that guy or anything did you Aubrey?"

Aubrey's senses were thrumming from the odd exchange. If she had felt like a teenager ten minutes ago, she felt like a superhero now. "Never seen him before in my life."

"Well I guess free stuff is always nice, even if it is from a creepy old man," Angela piped in. "You guys want to make up for it with a few rounds at the shooting gallery?" They nodded in agreement and headed to the far end of the midway, the bag of boxes bumping gently against Aubrey's thigh.

When Aubrey was back home and the glow from her kitchen light fixture seemed harsh and surreal against the darkness of the carnival, she sat at the table to examine her new gifts. The book from the library was present enough, but now to have two beautiful boxes quite literally handed to her the very next day was almost too much. *What is it? Give-random-stuff-to-Aubrey week?*

She laid the boxes in front of her on the table. As enamored as she had originally been with the stone box and its engraved flower design, it now seemed rather mediocre compared to the larger wooden box the old man had presented her with. She marveled once more at the pattern on the lid, running her finger over it and not feeling the definitions between the pieces of wood as she would have expected. She attempted to open the lid, but there were no hinges and no clasp. She thought perhaps it was a sliding lid, and tried pushing it every direction, but to no avail. *What good is a box if you can't even open it?* she thought with a sigh.

She turned the box over to examine the bottom. Nothing. With a shrug, Aubrey flicked off the light and went to bed.

Six

"She's got it alright, Max. Let's go get it." Leonard put down his binoculars. He didn't really need them. They had been able to park their van close enough to the girl's house without her noticing, and they could see straight into the kitchen. Still, he liked to use them. They gave him more of a sense of the mission.

"Nope. Too soon," Max replied.

"Are you kidding? It's right there! She's all alone, and I bet we could break in without even waking her."

His partner turned an icy blue eye to him. "You know as well as I do that we have to wait. For now, it's enough that we know she has it. It wouldn't do us any good to take it right now. It's not ready yet."

"Well I'm tired of waiting. We have been tracking that Source for years, and now that he has finally made his move, we just have to sit around some more?"

"Nobody said it would be easy or exciting, Leonard. At

least not yet."

Seven

The morning sunlight filtered into Aubrey's eyes, and she rolled away from it. She could smell coffee, and was grateful for the millionth time that her coffee pot had a timer on it. Coffee was yet another item she had switched to organic, and found it to be even more delicious.

Not quite as delicious as a Saturday morning, though. No alarm clock, no work, no boss breathing down her neck. Even as much as she liked most of her coworkers, it was nice to have a break from them, too.

When she was a kid, she would get up at the crack of dawn on Saturday mornings to watch cartoons. Her parents would stay in bed, and at the time she thought it was a courtesy to her, to give her some alone time. As an adult she realized they were taking advantage of the extra rest and relaxation. They trusted her, though, to be basically alone even at a very young age. She had learned to be very independent in her short time at the foster home, and her parents never tried to change that. Her mom made sure the box of Poptarts was set out on the counter and the milk was on the bottom shelf of the fridge, so she wouldn't have to wait for breakfast. Aubrey smiled to herself at the memories and wriggled further into the sheets.

There was a distinctive click from the kitchen. Her eyes flew open. Slowly, Aubrey climbed out of bed and grabbed the old baseball bat from behind the bedroom door, adrenaline surging through her body. She crept down the hall, bat in hand, sidestepping the squeaky board near the bathroom.

At the entrance to the living room she paused and looked around. Nothing. Everything was exactly as it should have been. The sunlight glinted off the antique vase on the corner table, and showed the thin film of dust on the television screen. Ok, all clear.

Aubrey slowly turned the corner into the kitchen. The baseball bat was poised above her shoulder, but again she saw nothing. She had been too full from the carnival food to worry about making dinner, and her pristine counter tops and sink proved it. The coffee pot gurgled at her. The boxes from the old man were on the table where she left them. She started to head for the garage, just to be sure, but turned to look at the boxes again.

The lid to the wooden box was open.

Someone had to have opened it. She examined the garage, the storage closet, and even went back down the hallway and looked in the shower. All of the doors and windows were secure. There was nobody here, and it didn't appear that there ever had been.

She returned to the kitchen to examine the box. The lid was indeed a sliding one, but it slid outwards to each side from the middle. Aubrey peered through the split lid. The interior of the box was lined in black velvet, and cradled an egg. It wasn't like an egg from the grocery store. It was quite a bit bigger, and the shell was a shining silver. Aubrey picked up the bauble and was surprised at its warmth. The egg was also quite heavy. *Sure hope it isn't made of lead.*

Looking back to the box, she could see there was still something in the space the egg had vacated. She reached in and pulled out a folded piece of parchment. In a loopy script,

It is time.

Aubrey quickly but gently put the egg back into the box, and ran back to her bedroom for the book.

Eight

If you are reading this, you have found yourself in the possession of a dragon egg. Many humans are of the belief that there is no magic left on Earth, but this quite simply is not true. In fact, Earth is home to the exact type of magic that a dragon needs when it is first starting its life.

Hatching your Dragonette requires great patience and care. You are capable of this or you would not have been chosen for this task. By now, you have the egg and you know it is time to start reading the book. It is very important that you still don't read ahead until it is time.

Oviparous Earth creatures keep their eggs warm, and dragon eggs are no different except for the fact that they require much more heat. The best method we can recommend for modern day Earth humans is to set your oven temperature to two-hundred degrees. Place the egg in the center of the oven, and leave the door halfway open.

When the shell of the egg begins to crack, remove the egg

from the oven...

Aubrey drummed her fingers on the kitchen counter. She had checked on the egg for the millionth time. She didn't really know how long this was going to take. She had read all through the chapter about hatching, but it never gave a time frame.

She contemplated going to the grocery store. She spent a lot of time there, especially since she was eating so many fresh fruits and vegetables. The organic ones in particular didn't stay fresh for long, so she only bought enough for a few days at a time. She picked up her purse and headed for the door, but as she reached for the doorknob she changed her mind. *What if it starts hatching while I'm gone?*

Her purse started to chirp and vibrate, so she reached in and pulled out her cell phone.

"Hey, girl, it's Betty! What are you up to today?"

Aubrey looked over her shoulder toward the kitchen. "Um, not a whole lot. You know, just hanging around the house. How about you?"

"Pretty much the same thing. I'm getting the house cleaned up today since my parents are coming over tomorrow for lunch."

"That's nice." Aubrey did think it was nice, but she would be a liar if she didn't admit she was a little jealous.

"Anyway, I wanted to call and make sure you were alright. Last night was kind of strange with that old man giving you that stuff."

"Yeah, I'm fine. It was strange, but I guess it was just his way of being nice." Aubrey ran a hand through her hair in frustration. She wished she could tell Betty about all this, but part of her still wondered if she was losing her sanity.

"Was there anything in the box?"

"What?"

"The wooden box. Was there anything in it? The old man seemed to think it was really important, so it made me wonder."

"Um, no. It was just a box. I, uh, think I'm going to keep it on my dresser with the flower box." She didn't like lying to Betty, but she really wasn't sure what else to say, especially if she didn't want to sound completely crazy.

"Cool. Well, I need to get the vacuum running so I'll let you go. Just thought I would check on you. See ya Monday!"

Well that was strange. Aubrey turned back to the oven and peered in again. The heat from the open door was making the kitchen almost unbearably hot. She grabbed a couple of oven mitts and pulled out the center rack to examine the egg more closely. There! A small but definite crack had developed along the left side of the egg.

Following the directions in the book and donning her oven mitts, she carefully lifted the egg out of the oven and placed it gently in its box. For a moment she worried the velvet wouldn't be able to withstand the heat from the egg, but she couldn't think of any better place to put it. She carried the box, egg inside, to the living room and set it on the corner table. She retrieved her cup of coffee from the kitchen and perched herself on the edge of the couch to watch.

The shell had changed color somewhat since she had put it in the oven. Before, it was a solid, brilliant silver. It was no longer quite so bright, but had gained an interesting iridescence and didn't seem quite so solid. As she studied the crack on the side, she noticed there was a tiny hole in the center of it. A minute, silver beak poked out of the hole for a moment, then disappeared.

Silver?

She consulted the book again to see if she had missed any information about what color the creature would be. Though the book was rather thick, the chapter about hatching seemed rather short, and had no information about the hue of her hatchling.

Aubrey brewed herself another pot of coffee, and spent the next several hours curled up to watch the show. For awhile, she thought about nothing but what was in front of her. She wasn't worried about work, or her medical issues, or her special diet. The only thing that bothered to crawl across her senses was the scent and taste of her coffee.

When the shell had come completely open, Aubrey couldn't believe what was before her eyes. The silver beak was the end of a small narrow face with big, intelligent eyes. It sat atop a long thin neck that led down to a perfectly proportioned set of wings, the skin on them nearly translucent. Muscular legs ended in tiny sharp talons, and a long tapered tail whipped softly back and forth.

What she had hatched, from a shiny silver egg, given to her by a strange old man, inside a box in the corner of her living room, was a dragon. A small, silver, baby dragon with scales and wings and everything. A dragon.

Nine

You will find that your newly hatched Dragonette does not need much care when it comes to his grooming and general maintenance.

Dragons are by nature a rather clean species. While it is not required to give him regular baths, don't be surprised to find him investigating your dishwater or inviting himself to share your shower. If he has regular opportunities to indulge in a bath when he wishes he will take better care of himself than any human could.

Your Dragonette is not a domesticated pet. He does not need his talons clipped or his teeth cleaned. He requires no special lotions, creams, oils, or medications...

Aubrey peered over the top of the book at the tiny silver creature perched on her table. He preened the underside of his scales, cleaning himself thoroughly. *Well, the book seems to be on track so far.*

Despite the presence of the book in her hands, Aubrey felt a growing sense of incompetence. She had a few pets growing up, but certainly nothing like this. She had begged her mother once for a cute little lizard she saw in the pet store. She could very clearly remember her mother bending over to peer into the cage at the little creature and frowning. "Reptiles just don't make good pets, Aubrey," she said. That was about the end of that, and Aubrey never asked again.

She and the dragon stared at each other for a few moments. Now that she did have her reptile, she just wasn't sure what to do with it.

"Well, I suppose the first thing I ought to do is give you a name," she said. "Um, Jack?"

The dragon cocked his head to one side and blinked a few times.

"Max?"

Blink.

"Draco?"

She could have sworn she heard a snort of derision.

"Alright, let's see what the book says about this." She skimmed through the table of contents, but nowhere did she find a chapter on naming your mystical creature. He was silver, and that was a start, but it was somehow more than just silver. It was almost a liquid type of silver, like mercury. She thought back to her high school chemistry class and what she knew about mercury. There wasn't much information still in there, other than the chemical symbol was Hg.

"Hugo?"

The Dragonette stretched his wings out as far as they could go and fluttered them about. He stepped off the table and onto the arm of the couch, shoving his head underneath

Audrey's chin. She couldn't help but laugh.

"Okay, okay! I guess I found the right one!" She laughed and ran a cautious finger down the length of the dragon's neck. His scales were smooth and slippery like a snake's, but he felt more solid underneath. He arched his neck toward her hand for more. Pulses of energy tickled her palms and shot up through her wrists. "Let's figure out what to feed you." Hugo clambered up to the back of the couch and perched above her shoulder as she picked the book back up.

Ten

Now that your Dragonette has hatched, your job as a foster parent has truly begun.

Dragons are by nature carnivores. While they do not require sheep or villagers as you might think (unless, of course, you have immediate access to such things), they do need a steady diet of fresh meat, eggs, and even a few fruits and vegetables. All meat must be thoroughly cooked until your Dragonette is old enough to do it himself, which will come quite some time before he is actually able to hunt. In short: be prepared for a large grocery bill.

The kind of meat is not as important as the freshness. Your Dragonette will let you know if the meat you offer is past his preferred expiration date. If he turns his nose up at what you offer, do not try to force him. It is also extremely important that you do not feed your dragon any canned or processed food.

Although your Dragonette no longer requires the warmth

of the oven, he will still need a source of heat...

"Alright, Hugo. Let's see what the fridge has to offer." Aubrey got up off the couch and headed for the kitchen. Hugo watched her for a moment, then clambered to the floor to follow.

"You're very impressive, Hugo. I can't believe you move around that quickly after hatching."

She scanned the contents of her fridge. According to the book, Hugo needed the same type of food Aubrey was buying for herself anyway. She found an organic steak she had picked up yesterday. "Alright, buddy. Looks like this should do."

Aubrey paused as she took the steak out of the packaging. The book said she had to cook it, but what was the right way to cook dragon food? Smiling to herself, she cut the steak into small bites and lit the gas stove. Holding the steak one piece at a time with a pair of tongs, she singed it over the blue flame. It was as close to how he would end up cooking it himself as she could imagine.

She placed the steak pieces on a paper plate on the floor in front of Hugo. The tiny dragon inched towards the plate cautiously, nose in the air as he sniffed at the steak. He dragged one bite of the steak off the plate onto the floor, sniffed at it some more, then gobbled it up. He dragged the next piece onto the floor.

"Okay, so you don't like plates. Point taken, but that's going to be hell to clean up all the time." Hugo glanced at her out of the corner of his eye, but continued to work on the steak.

"Alright, now I just have to figure out what the heck I'm

going to do with you while I'm at work." She couldn't possibly let a dragon, baby or not, wander around her house for eight hours while she worked. The book said he would need someplace warm, and that was definitely the kitchen. The way the sun shone through the windows in the afternoon made it by far the warmest room in the house.

Rummaging through the garage, she found an old plastic dog crate. She had picked it up at a yardsale last summer when she was thinking about getting a dog. She thought it would keep her place from seeming so lonely, but she hadn't been able to bring herself to actually do it. The book said he needed a space that wasn't too confining, but the crate was quite a bit bigger than the dragon. At least if he got out he would be stuck in the kitchen, where he could probably do the least amount of damage.

Eleven

"He hatched this morning, sir."

"Good. Continue to keep an eye on him." The darkly robed figured did not bother to turn away from the window.

"Is there anything else, sir?"

"No, that's all for now, Leonard. We will move when it's time."

Twelve

Aubrey sat in the break room with her head propped on her hand. She had spent most of the night worrying about Hugo. In some ways, he was worse than having a baby at home. She had gotten up to check on him almost on the hour, and it was only a few of those hours into the night before he had the plastic dog crate in pieces on the kitchen floor. She could only hope he wouldn't manage to work his way out of the kitchen before she got home from work.

"Hey, Aubrey. How was your weekend?"

She had been trying to avoid most of her coworkers today, but Ben in particular. She was going to have to start eating lunch at her desk. "Um, pretty good, I guess. How about yours?" *Ugh, I have got to stop being so polite.*

"Oh, it was great!" He sat down across the table from her and unwrapped a sandwich. "We had a pretty big turnout for LARP. You should have been there."

"Oh." Aubrey wasn't sure what else to say for a moment.

With a baby dragon at home in her kitchen, she had completely forgotten about Ben's invitation. Not that she had really intended to go anyway. "Well, I'm glad it went well for you."

"Not that crap again, Ben." Angela sat down next to Ben and quite literally looked down her nose at him. "You are so lame." She cracked open a diet shake.

"Thank you so much for your delightful input, Angela. The funny thing is, nobody asked for it." Ben took a swig of his Coke.

Angela was not about to let it go. "Listen, Ben. We're adults here, not junior high nerds. How can you trot around in tights all weekend and not want to kill yourself by Monday morning?"

"It's called escapism, and I don't exactly 'trot around in tights'. It's not any different than someone going to the movies or reading a good book."

"It's stupid, is what it is, right Aubrey?" Angela turned her steely blue gaze to Aubrey. "Wow, you look awful."

"Gee, thanks. Rough night."

"Anyway, tell him how silly his little plays are." Angela smugly sipped her shake with a sidelong glance to Ben and a smirk on the corners of her mouth.

Aubrey hesitated. Ben's perspective was a spin she hadn't thought about before. She remembered how much the books she read as a child changed her life. She would imagine herself in those stories for hours, and the only real difference was that she did it alone in her bedroom instead of with a bunch of other people in the park. "Don't you think you're being a little harsh, Angela?" She thought she saw Ben look at her with a glimmer of hope in his eyes.

"Seriously, Aubrey? You mean to tell me that you don't think it's odd for grown men to run around the park saving princesses?"

Aubrey just shrugged. "I guess if the princesses need saving…"

"Well, whatever. If you dorks feel like slaying dragons I guess I will just leave you to it." Angela and her diet shake breezed out of the break room.

Aubrey turned a sharp glance to Ben. "Do you guys really pretend to slay dragons?"

Ben shook his head as he finished his bite of chicken. "No, that's just what people who don't know any better think. Most of the people in our group are actually really into dragons."

"Really." She picked through her unsalted cashews idly and felt the awkward silence drift down around them.

Ben finally broke the gap in conversation. "Listen, Aubrey. I appreciate you taking my side there. I really don't care what Angela or anybody else thinks of me, and I know you aren't interested in what I like to do, but what you did was awesome."

"It's no big deal, Ben. That's just Angela being her snobby self. I like her on some level, but I don't think there's much call for the way she was treating you."

"No, it is a big deal. I know I'm a nerd, and a lot of people can't stand that. But I like being a nerd. I learned a long time ago to be happy with who I am."

Aubrey found a genuine smile creeping across her face for Ben. "That's great."

"How's your dragon book coming along? Any good?"

"Better than you would ever believe."

"I don't know about that. I've read quite a bit of fantasy fiction myself."

Aubrey smiled at him sleepily. "I had no idea you were into all this stuff. I thought you were just into computers."

"Yeah, well, I know people like Angela think it's juvenile, but it's fun. And I had no idea you were into it either. The books, I mean."

"It's a nice escape, just like you said. But to be honest with you, it's not the kind of thing I normally read. I haven't been into stuff like that for a very, very long time."

"Why's that?"

"Um," Aubrey paused, staring down past her cashews and into the past. She hadn't told many people about her childhood. Even Betty knew only the very basics. "I guess I just lost my sense of fantasy, you know? Disillusioned by reality and all that."

Ben nodded his head slowly. Well, hey, at least you're rediscovering it now, right? Getting to know yourself again?"

Aubrey snapped her head back up to look at him sharply.

"What? Did I say something wrong?" Ben asked.

"Um, no. I just...I hadn't thought about it like that. Not at all."

"Listen, I've got to get back to work. I promise you I won't bother you with invitations on the weekends any more, but the offer is open if you ever change your mind."

"You know, I think I just might take you up on it this time."

Thirteen

You will very quickly find that your Dragonette knows a lot about you. Dragons and humans have had a magical bond for so many ages that dragons are now born with a certain innate knowledge of humankind. To our species this seems impossible, but to them it is only natural.

While your Dragonette will not be able to use human speech until he is mature, he will understand you almost immediately. Be patient and watch his body language closely. Your Dragonette will be sure to find his own ways of expressing himself to you.

Along with language, dragons are surprisingly aware of human physiology...

As Aubrey drove home from work, her mind consistently wandered back to Ben. She hadn't planned on going with him on the weekend. The words just seemed to fall out of her mouth. And once they did she really wasn't sure what he would say. Surely someone she had pointedly ignored since he came to the company would jump at the opportunity to turn her down, and she was quite surprised when he didn't.

"Really?" he had asked. "I mean, that's great. It starts fairly early. I can pick you up around nine."

Aubrey's heart pounded in her chest. How the heck would she hide Hugo from him if he picked her up? "No! I mean, um, I can just meet you there." With that obstacle out of the way, she had the rest of the week to stress about exactly what she was supposed to do with herself at LARP.

Her mind, for a moment, flickered to the cancer support group that the nurse at the doctor's office had told her about. With everything that had happened this weekend, she had nearly forgotten it, and at least forgot it enough that she hadn't thought about going. Even though she couldn't see Ben tonight, she didn't take the turn for the community center where the support group was held. She imagined herself sitting in a circle of chairs in a drab room, introducing herself and listening to everyone's sad stories. She shuddered, and pressed the accelerator a little harder.

Back at home, Aubrey carefully opened the kitchen door and peered in. Hugo was curled up in a patch of sunlight in front of the sliding glass door, and looked up at her sleepily as she came in. There were a few scratches on the kitchen door, but all in all the place seemed to be in one piece.

"You hungry, buddy? At least, for something other than plastic?" Aubrey frowned at the remnants of the dog crate sticking out of the trash can, and started making his dinner right away. She had left him a good-size meal in the morning, but an eight-hour work day had to be an eternity for him.

Hugo seemed to get very excited as she pulled food out of

the fridge. He flapped his little wings, made minute hissy noises, and if dragons paced he certainly was doing it.

"I know, I know! I'm working on it! But until you can cook it yourself you are going to have to be patient with me. Last I checked, I didn't breathe fire."

Aubrey's dinner of free-range chicken with Normandy vegetables seemed to be a hit with her new foster child. He was chomping down on it before she could get it all on his plate. When she curled up on the couch to watch some after-dinner television, he didn't hesitate to make his way onto her lap to cuddle.

"You are far friendlier than I ever imagined a reptile could be."

Hugo lifted his head off her chest and gave her an odd look.

"Now, now, I'm not saying you are any ordinary reptile. Not by any means."

Hugo lay his head back down with a snort, and Aubrey turned on the television. She flipped through a few stations, trying to find something worth watching. She paid far too much money for there not to be anything on. Finally settling on an old sitcom rerun, she looked down to find Hugo staring at her intently.

"What's wrong?"

He continued to stare, then started to weave his head back and forth on its long neck. He stopped on her left side, and dove into her armpit.

"Just what the heck are you doing?"

Hugo had turned his body so that he was facing her side underneath her arm. He seemed to be sniffing the air intently.

"Are you trying to tell me I need to take a shower? Do I

stink?" Aubrey tried to get the Dragonette out from under her arm and back onto her lap, but he only wedged himself in more firmly against the arm of the couch. When she reached for him a second time, he batted her hand away.

"Watch the attitude, Mr. Grouchypants!"

Hugo ignored her and commenced his sniffing, but his breathing became deeper. Aubrey could feel a warmth that started under her arm and spread throughout her body. Hugo laid his hands on her and wiggled his talons almost imperceptibly. They made the tiniest pinpricks in her skin, but she didn't move. Whatever he was up to, Hugo was determined. A blue light shimmered around them, then sparked out in great sweeping arcs on her body. Aubrey was paralyzed with awe and disbelief. The dragon's eyes were closed now, as though he was concentrating on making the blue light. Hypnotized, Aubrey couldn't take her eyes off Hugo's face. Pulses of warmth swept through her body, and she felt her muscles relaxing involuntarily.

Just as quickly as he had started, it was over. The light dissipated and Hugo opened his eyes. The warm sensation that had filled her body just moments before was gone, and it left her with an intense chill. She grabbed the throw blanket off the back of the couch and arranged it over her before she managed to look back at the odd little creature that had just done this, whatever it was, to her.

He was still wedged between her and the arm of the couch, and the look on his face made Aubrey think he might be just as confused as she was.

"What on Earth did you just do?"

He blinked at her a couple times, then crawled back onto her lap. He curled himself up into a tiny silver ball, and promptly fell asleep.

"Weirdo."

Fourteen

The sunlight dripped down through the trees and dappled the park with leopard spots as Aubrey looked for a parking space. She didn't frequent the park often, but had certainly never seen so many people here. Cars were even pulled over onto the grass. She took a deep breath as she put the car in park and tried to calm her stomach. She was not good at new things.

She had spent a good hour the night before just trying to decide what to wear. Obviously she wasn't going to be dressed up as one of the characters; she was just there as a spectator. But should she go casual with a t-shirt? Or a little more dressed up with that cute button down blouse? She wasn't even sure what kind of impression she was looking to make upon Ben. Were they just friends? Did she want something more? Did *he* want something more, or was she reading too much into it? She finally settled on jeans and a lace-trimmed tank top. Casual, but cute. Last minute, she grabbed her old Celtic medallion necklace from the back of her jewelry armoire. *I haven't worn this thing since high school.*

Knights and princesses swarmed around her as she made her way to the center of the park. Ben said he would probably be there before she was, but with half of the people here dressed in chainmail she didn't think she would ever find him. A throne was set up under a huge oak tree, but it was empty. Aubrey settled on one of the crude benches that had been set up in a semicircle for spectators. She wasn't about to wander all over the place like an idiot looking for him.

After a few minutes she pulled her phone out to send him a text message, and at least let him know she had shown up. *Do kings carry their cell phones on them?*

"Pardon me, m'lady, but what kind of sorcery are you using?"

Startled, Aubrey looked up to find a handsome man smiling down at her. He, like the others, was quite covered in chainmail, but he wore a red tunic with a gold dragon emblazoned on the front. It was when she saw the thick gold circlet on his head that she realized it was Ben.

"Oh! Uh, hi! I didn't see you. Well, I might have, but I didn't recognize you without your glasses."

"They kind of clash with my costume. And I was talking to the gamemaster."

"Who?"

"The gamemaster is the guy who orchestrates the whole thing and determines the majority of what happens."

"Oh," Aubrey replied, feeling a bit stupid. "Is there anything I'm supposed to do while I'm here?"

Ben smiled, and Aubrey felt her stomach leap up a bit.

"Just make sure your cell phone is on silent, to keep the authenticity as much as we can. Other than that, just enjoy." He looked like he was about to walk away, but then he paused. "Um, there is one more thing."

"Yes?"

He cleared his throat and his cheeks reddened a bit. "M'lady, would you grant me your favor for the tournament?"

"The tournament? You mean, like jousting?"

"Nothing so grand as that. We don't have the room or the horses, but we do have swordfights, archery contests and the like."

"And even King Arthur himself deigns to compete?"

"Round Table and all that."

"Um," Aubrey looked down at her outfit. What was she supposed to use as a favor? She remembered from those days as a child that a lady would tie her colors on a knight's arm, and wished it had been cool enough to wear a scarf. She took off her necklace and wrapped it around his upper arm, reclasping it in the back. The hard bicep under the armor surprised her. She had managed to keep the medallion pendant right at the front, dangling down over the other loops of chain and gleaming against his mail. "Will that work?"

Ben looked down at her handiwork. "Aubrey," he breathed. His eyes met hers, and she nearly fell into them. "It's perfect." And he was off across the grass towards his throne, the pendant glittering in the sun.

A couple hours later, Aubrey found herself a bit sad that everything was over. There had indeed been several swordfights and an archery competition, which Ben did quite well in. There was even an elaborate play involving King

Arthur and his knights on part of their quest for the Holy Grail. It was clear now that they were wrapping things up, as Ben was on his throne and thanking all of his guests and courtiers.

About a dozen other spectators were scattered on the benches around her. "I've been trying to figure out all morning what that is on the king's arm," she heard a woman's voice say.

"I'm not sure. I've never seen him wear it before. The only thing I could guess would be a lady's favor." This voice was most definitely male.

"Pfft!" retorted the first voice. "I've never seen Ben do anything of the sort. Hell, I even *offered* him my bandana back in the spring and he wouldn't take it!"

Aubrey resisted the urge to turn around and peek at them, but she could feel a cat-that-ate-the-canary smile creep across her face.

"Now, don't get so bent out of shape," the man replied. "Things change. Even Ben can't be a loner forever. Here, he's coming. You can ask him yourself."

"Maybe I will."

Indeed, Ben's reign was over and he was heading straight for the spectators. Not for the first time that day, Aubrey felt her heart pounding in her chest. He held out his hand to help her up off the bench, and she could hear a deflated sigh from the woman behind her.

"Aubrey, I'm so glad you came. I hope you weren't too bored." He didn't let go of her hand.

"Not in the slightest, actually. It was definitely not what I was expecting."

"Will you walk with me back to my car so I can get all of

this off? It's not too bad to wear it out here, but chainmail kind of sucks when you get into a hot car." At her nod, he tucked her hand into the crook of his elbow and escorted her towards the parking lot, and she didn't mind the press of the chainmail or the muscles underneath it against her arm. He gestured toward an older SUV. "My loyal steed awaits." He opened the back and began stripping off his costume, quickly transforming from King Arthur into the Ben she was more familiar with. As he pulled off his tunic and chainmail, Aubrey couldn't help but admire the sinewy muscles that were normally hidden so well behind his computer nerd façade. *Wow, sexy nerd alert.*

He looked at her and smiled. "I hope I honored you with my efforts on the field today."

She tried not to blush, and her cheeks were going to hurt if she didn't stop smiling soon. "Indeed, good sir."

Ben leaned back against the bumper to change into sneakers. "I really do mean it, Aubrey. I am so glad you're here. It meant a lot to me. I know I spent most of this time 'trotting around in tights' as Angela would say, so I wasn't hanging out with you, but I'd like to. I want to know more about you. Can I take you out to lunch?"

I want to know more about you. It echoed in her head, and the smile faded quickly from her lips. He couldn't possibly know more about her, about her true secret. He might call the cops, or animal control, or sell him as the main attraction at a fantasy convention, or just run screaming for the hills. A baby dragon at home was a bit more than "Oh, gee, I guess I should have told you I'm a crazy cat lady." She could feel the great yawning pit of loneliness open up underneath her once again. Her mouth didn't seem to want to work anymore, and she just shook her head. The disappointed look on his face was quickly blurred as tears stung her eyes, and she turned away toward her car.

"Aubrey, please don't go."

But she only walked faster, heading home toward Hugo, the only companion she would probably ever have.

Fifteen

The slightly flickering fluorescent light above her desk was starting to get to her. She checked the time at the bottom corner of her computer monitor: only fifteen more minutes to go and she was home free. Even her work couldn't keep her attention today.

"Hey girl!" Betty's face came peeking over the top of the cubicle. I haven't talked to you much this week. Everything going ok?"

Aubrey smiled. "Yeah, could be worse I guess."

"Mmm...I heard something along those lines."

"As in?"

"I heard you had a date with a certain nerd I know."

"I don't know that you can actually classify it as a date..."

"Close enough! I can't believe you didn't tell me! I had to overhear it from Angela!"

"How did she find out? I mean, not that I care, but I didn't mention it to her." Aubrey stacked up her file folders and put her pens in the drawer.

"Silly girl. You can't exactly agree to go out with a guy out in the break room and not expect everybody to know about it within a few hours. So did you go to his nerd thing?"

"It's really not that nerdy. It's pretty cool. There are some talented actors in his group."

"Oooo....sounds like someone is getting sweet on someone! I'm glad, though. Ben has been wild about you ever since he started working here. And I bet all the other nerds are crazy jealous of him."

"No, Betty, it's really not like that. I just went with him as friends," Aubrey protested. "I don't have space in my life right now for anything more than that."

"Uh, huh. Sure. Whatever you say, girl." Betty flicked her gaze over Aubrey's shoulder. "Boss man's coming!" She disappeared back over the cubicle wall before Aubrey had any more chances to make her case.

Aubrey turned back to her desk and tried to look busy. She didn't have much she could accomplish in the last few minutes of the day, but she knew Mr. Milner thought every second of work time should count. He was known to patrol the offices at the end of the day to make sure nobody was skipping out early. She could hear him pause behind her at the entrance to her cubicle.

"Miss Goodknight?"

She turned around in her chair. "Yes, Mr. Milner?"

"You did a good job on the monthly report." His eyes were focused not on Aubrey but on the rollers on the bottom of her chair. "I'd like you to give a presentation on it at the next board meeting."

"Thank you, Mr. Milner. I would be delighted."

"Yes, well," he made a dismissive gesture with his hand.

Now was as good a time as ever. "Mr, Milner, I need to ask for another day off. I know I just had one, but they had to schedule another appointment for me. It won't be for a few days yet, but I wanted to give you as much notice as possible."

His hard little eyes now stared straight into hers. He had the power again. "Is this going to be a continuing trend with you? I don't want to bring a new person in on the board meetings if she's just going to flake out on me every time she has her period."

Pig. "No, sir. It shouldn't be an issue." *At least I hope not.*

"Very well then. Notify Kay of the exact date so she can put it on the calendar." Without so much as a have-a-nice-evening, Mr. Milner turned on his heel and moved on through the cubicles.

Aubrey finished straightening up her desk and headed for the elevator. She managed to squeeze in with everyone else that was trying to leave the fifth floor. A couple of the women chatted, but mostly everyone watched the floor levels tick down, eager to get home. She wondered what they were going home to. Some of them probably had spouses and children that would be waiting for them at the table, eager to discuss their days and plans for the future. Others quite likely came home to an empty apartment, and would sit down to a microwaved meal in front of the TV. She knew, though, that she was the only one going home to a needy dragon. She had never felt so special and so sad at the same time.

Ben was waiting for her in the lobby. She tried to pretend she didn't see him, but he wasn't going to let her get by with that. He stopped her as she headed to the front door.

"Aubrey, please talk to me. I don't know what I did to offend you, but whatever it is I am so sorry."

She looked up at him. He was now completely back to being just a regular guy at the office. His white dress shirt hid his well-toned abs and nice biceps that she had gotten a peek of as he had removed his chainmail. There was no crown or sword to make him any different from anyone else here. He had his glasses back on, but his green eyes stared down at her with an intensity that she was sure his computer monitor would be jealous of. She sighed and looked away.

"Ben, it's just…It's just complicated." She could see that most of the crowd of employees had filtered out the door and into the parking lot and wished she was headed out there with them. At least nobody would be gawking at them.

"What is it? You're married?"

"Ha! Not even close." She looked back at him, and saw that her comment was only going to make him pursue this further.

"Aubrey, please. I don't like putting myself out there like this, but I really like you. If you don't like me back, that's okay, but just please tell me what I did wrong. I had such a good time with you, but then it was like all of a sudden everything changed on me. I can make up for whatever I did if it would make it better."

"Ben, you didn't do anything wrong. I'm sorry. I don't know how to explain it. I guess you could say I just have a lot of baggage right now."

"I've always wanted a new luggage set."

"Funny. I wish it was that simple."

"It's okay, I won't tell anyone you're part of the witness

protection program. There, at least I got a smile out of you."

   "I've got to go. I'll talk to you later."

Sixteen

Many humans are familiar with dragons as fire-breathing creatures. While this is very common, the ice dragons are, for obvious reasons, not fire breathers. (If you believe your Dragonette to be a rare ice dragon, please see Appendix A.)

You must take precautions when your Dragonette begins showing signs of creating fire. Even while very young, dragons contain a rather large amount of explosive energy. Be diligent in protecting your home. Never let your Dragonette practice around large flammable objects, such as curtains, couches, and beds. It is advisable to disable your smoke alarms. They will be going off quite often as your Dragonette practices.

Be sure to give your dragon lots of opportunities to practice. Let him cook you dinner, and light the grill or campfire. Give him practice on precision by lighting candles. The more outlets for flame he has the less likely he is to accidentally burn your precious possessions with pent-up flame frustrations.

Be patient with him as he learns this skill. There is very little you can do to help him with it other than offering encouragement and opportunity.

The same advice goes for flying. When you notice that your Dragonette is interested, give him plenty of encouragement and space. If you live in town, you will need to find a place where your Dragonette will have plenty of room to spread his wings without being in the view of outsiders.

Fire usually comes at about the same time that your Dragonette will start trying to fly...

After successfully avoiding Ben all day, the empty feeling she'd had in the elevator had turned to eagerness for the solitude of her home. At the very least, solitude from other humans, who only seemed to make life harder. Since her outing with Ben, she had started eating her lunch at her desk instead of the break room. That was one way to keep Ben from trying to talk to her again. She wasn't too thrilled about the idea of hearing criticism from Angela over the whole thing, either. The only person she did still have to deal with was Betty, and that wasn't so bad. She considered Betty a good friend, but even she couldn't know the real reason she didn't want to get close to Ben.

"Are you going to stay at your desk all day?" Betty had asked her that afternoon. This time she had actually come all the way around the cubicle wall, and Aubrey admired her floral chiffon dress and platform heels. Betty looked like a pin up picture in person. It would be nice to look so cute so easily.

"Pretty much. It's just easier."

"You don't think you should talk to Ben?"

Aubrey sighed for the billionth time in a week. "I don't know, maybe."

"If you're not interested, you should just tell him. He seems like a nice guy, and it won't hurt him as bad if you're just honest with him."

"I don't know if I can be honest with him. I don't know what I want. I guess I'm just scared."

"Well, I know I can't tell you what you should do, but he's been looking like a sad puppy all week. And honey, he's probably just as scared as you are."

Aubrey shook her head. "I wouldn't be so sure about that. In the little bit of time I've spent with him, he's a lot more assertive than I ever would have expected out of an IT guy."

Betty didn't push her anymore, but Aubrey couldn't get it off her mind. When she got home, Hugo was more than happy to try to distract her, but she could only smile sadly at him while he rubbed his head on her chin and flapped his wings at her. Even having a dragon at home couldn't pull her away from the ache she felt in her heart.

"I guess I'm just always meant to be alone, buddy." She and Hugo were curled up on the floor in front of the couch, watching TV. He had grown fast in the last week, and was a little bigger every day. He easily rivaled a medium size dog. Well, a dog with wings anyway. He nuzzled his head into her cheek. "Yeah, yeah. I've got you, anyway. You're the only family I've had in a long time. I'm not ungrateful, but do you have any idea how hard it is to have a dragon and not be able to tell anybody? At least you won't be flying away from me anytime soon, right?"

At this, Hugo leapt up from their cozy spot on the floor and shot into the kitchen. Aubrey headed after him, and peered through the kitchen door. His shrill screech echoed from somewhere above her, and she looked up to see him perched on the top of the cabinets. "What are you doing up there?" He cocked his head and fluttered his wings, as if to say, "Isn't it obvious?" He spread his wings crisply straight and dove from the cabinet top. Aubrey watched with her heart in her throat as he swooped gracefully before hitting the floor. Unfortunately, he put too much energy in the uptake, hit the light fixture and fell to the floor.

"Hugo!" Aubrey ran to the baby dragon. In the time it took her just to cross her kitchen, he was picking himself up and shaking out his wings. "You have got to be more careful, baby!"

Hugo, like a bratty child, wouldn't look at her. He stretched his wings out and dug his talons into the rug, preparing for the next flight.

"Well don't do it in here, for Pete's sake! You'll hurt yourself. Or my furniture."

This time he did deign to give her a glance, and shot a puff of smoke through his nostrils.

"Oh, no."

Just then, a knock came at the front door. Hugo snapped to attention, his nostrils flaring. He dashed from the kitchen as quickly as he had come into it.

"No, you don't, you guard dragon!" Aubrey scrambled after him, and found him sniffing along the threshold of the front door. She scooped him up, no easy task at this point, and dumped him unceremoniously back in the kitchen. "You stay in here."

Moving back to the front door, she only had a moment to wonder at who was on the other side. She opened the door to find a handsome geek on her front step, his fist raised in preparation to knock again. "Ben? What are you doing here?"

Ben quickly turned his knocking gesture into a grand bow. "I humbly beg your forgiveness, m'lady, but it seems that I forgot to give you this." He pulled her medallion necklace out of his pocket and held it out to her. "I'm sorry to bother you, and I know you don't want to talk to me, but I did at least have to return it to you."

"Why didn't you just give it back to me at the office?"

"You didn't really give me a chance."

"Oh." Aubrey took the necklace from him. "I appreciate it." She could hear Hugo scratching at the kitchen door.

"It's a beautiful necklace. Where did you get it?"

Aubrey looked down at the medallion in her hand and remembered the Renaissance fair her foster father had taken her to. "I, um, I've had it a long time. My dad bought it for me in junior high."

"Oh, wow. In that case I'm really glad I returned it to you. It must be special to you."

"Yes, well..." Aubrey stared down at the Celtic knot in her palm. She knew Ben was trying to make more conversation with her, but the knot in her throat was even bigger than the one in her hand.

"Look, I know what your answer will probably be, but there's a really good band playing at The Stag and Hound tomorrow night, and I..."

Hugo burst out from the kitchen, all claws and wings and growls. "Hugo, no!" Aubrey cried as she slammed the door in

Ben's face. The dragon scrabbled around her legs, trying desperately to get to the door. She pushed him behind her with her foot and opened the door a crack. "Look, Ben, I'm sorry but..."

"What the heck was that?"

"What was what?"

"Was that your dog?"

"Um, yes. Yes! He's my dog. Hugo's my dog. Shit!" Hugo had escaped from behind her foot and was grappling his way up the curtains of the picture window. "So, I need to go, okay?"

"Uh, ok. But, um, would you go with me to the see the band tomorrow night?"

Aubrey slammed the door a second time and pulled Hugo away from the window just as he was sinking his talons into the sill. She cracked the door once again. "Yes I'll go with you to see the band but I need to take care of this right now so I'll meet you at the office after work okay? Bye!" This time when she shut the door she latched the dead bolt, and sank to the floor to catch her breath. She could hear Ben's car door shut and his ignition start. Hugo curled up in her lap and breathed a puff of smoke at her. "You have got to be the most rotten little dragon I've ever gotten a hold of."

Seventeen

Aubrey took the elevator down to the lower level, and couldn't remember ever having done so before. When she opened the door marked "IT", she was taken aback by the amount of equipment that had been crammed into the room. Servers were stacked up on top of each other, with various cables sprouting out of them like snakes on Medusa's head. These snakes, however, continued down onto the floor and undulated benignly around boxes and desks. The smell of electronics and reams of paper permeated the room. Ben sat at a desk in the middle of it all, bristling with monitors.

"Ben?"

"Oh, hey Aubrey. Welcome to Nerd HQ."

She smiled. "I'm pretty sure I just stepped into a sci-fi movie."

"Not exactly the genre I prefer, but I'll take what I can get. What's up?"

She spun her ring on her finger and chewed her lip a little.

"I just...I just wanted to make sure we actually were on for tonight. I mean, I was kind of rude to you last night when you dropped by, and I'm really sorry. I have a lot of lot of things going on."

Ben flicked off his monitors and came around the desk, smiling. "It can't be that bad, right? As long as you don't have a shrine of your ex's preserved parts in a closet somewhere, then I think we're okay. You ready to go?"

He walked her out to the parking lot and opened the door of his coupe hybrid for her. He climbed in the driver's seat.

"Sorry, I tend to leave the Ferrari at home when I'm working."

Aubrey swung her head to look at him incredulously and saw the smirk on his face. She laughed. "I was starting to think I work for the wrong department!"

"The SUV is great for LARP weekends, but I like something more practical for the commute."

When they had settled in at the bar, Aubrey found herself staring into her foamy beer, unsure of what to say. *I have really gone and made things awkward. Good job, Aubrey.*

"Um, I probably shouldn't start the evening off this way, but I can't help it." Ben fiddled with the corner of the napkin under his beer mug. "Why are you here? It's not that I'm not thrilled, but I can't help but wonder when I'm going to wake up. Or when someone is going to jump out and tell me I'm on Candid Camera. It's just that you seem to keep changing your mind about me."

Aubrey looked up abruptly from her drink, and realized her mouth was agape. She promptly shut it. "I can see why you would say that. I've been a pretty awful person lately."

"No! No, I wasn't trying to say that. I just...uh...aw

crap." He slumped back in his seat. "I'm just trying to say that I'm having a hard time fathoming this. Wow, I sound like such a desperate dork."

"It's ok. I mean, no you don't, but I understand what you mean. I know I've made things awkward between us and I'm sorry."

"Don't be sorry." He smiled at her and held up his mug. "To unusual coworker relationships!"

Aubrey followed suit and held her mug level with his. "And the awkward silences that surely will follow!" They tapped their mugs and drank.

Wiping a little foam from the corner of her lip, Aubrey realized this wasn't exactly consistent with her organic diet. She sighed a little, but decided to let it go. *No worse than the carnival food.* "You know, in all seriousness, I think I've just had a big change in perspective lately. My life has changed a lot just in the last few days. I don't really understand it all myself, but things are different now."

"Cancer will do that to you."

Aubrey stared at him indignantly. "Betty said she wouldn't tell!"

"I would be willing to gamble that she didn't."

"But she's the only person I told."

"Hey, it's a big office, lots of cubicles. Someone was probably closer than you realized when you told her, and, well, word travels ridiculously fast around there."

"Like how everyone most likely already knows we're out together?"

"Yeah, like that." He paused. "I hope you don't mind. That people know about us, I mean."

"Well, I'm guessing the fact that you are even here means

you don't mind about the cancer thing, so I think I can tolerate a little bit of office gossip."

"Mind? I'd have to be a pretty big jerk to turn you down for a drink just because you've got a medical issue going on. And I'm not trying to be nosey here, but is everything okay?"

"I don't really know yet. I don't want to bore you with the details..."

Ben reached across the table and put his hand on hers. "C'mon, bore me."

Her stomach fluttered at his touch, but she tried to get her wits together. "Well, I'm supposed to have a body scan to see if the cancer is anywhere else before they start operating."

"I don't mean to be too forward, but do you need anyone to go with you?"

Ben was looking more and more like the knight in shining armor he portrayed on weekends. "I appreciate it. But I think this is something I want to do myself. I gotta have a little bit of mystery about myself, right? Besides, hospital gowns aren't exactly flattering."

A couple beers later, Aubrey found herself feeling deliriously good. She had stopped thinking about the lump and its potential consequences. The band really was good, and she let herself enjoy the music. For the first time in as long as she could remember, she felt completely relaxed. The band had taken a break, and she was ready to talk more. "Ben, what would you do if you had a dragon?"

"You mean, like a real one?"

"Yeah." She could tell she was smiling too much, but she couldn't help it. Most people would have thought that was about the strangest first-official-date question she could have asked, but Ben rolled right with it.

"Wow. I don't really know, I guess. It would be a hard thing to hide from the public. Talk about your office gossip."

"True. Couldn't really tell anybody. Although I'm sure you would want to, right?"

Ben nodded. "Of course. How could you not want to share something as incredible as that?"

"Mmm...how not indeed." The corners of her mouth kept turning up on their own accord.

"Are you okay, Aubrey? Do I need to cut you off?"

She blinked a few times, trying to get the fog out of her eyes and wondered why that always happened when she drank. Her body felt light and comfortable, but her head was very clear. "I'm better than I have been in a long time. I'm working on it. I'm a bit of a lightweight when it comes to drinking, though." She smiled some more.

Ben smiled back, but his eyes traveled over her shoulder and the smile quickly faded. "You know, that guy in the corner has been watching us most of the time that we've been here. No, don't look! It's creepy."

She shrugged. "Probably just some loser that lives in his mother's basement and can't stand the thought of two people having a nice evening."

"I live in my mother's basement," Ben replied. Aubrey nearly choked on her beer. "I'm kidding! I most definitely have my own place. I might be a computer nerd and do LARP on the weekends, but I pay my own rent, and that makes it okay. And I don't have any Star Wars bed sheets anymore, either."

She laughed, and it felt good. "You are too awesome."

"Too awesome? Does that mean I'm awesome enough that if I asked you to go out with me again you would say yes?" He studied her face, and she felt herself sober up a little. Just enough to wonder what she was doing. Did he really like her? Where was this going? Questions, questions, questions. Ben grabbed her hand and held it tightly between both of his. "Aubrey, please don't clam up on me again. I know I haven't known you very long but I know that look on your face. You're getting ready to tell me no, and despite the way this makes me sound I really couldn't stand that."

The wavering in her brain was intense. So intense that there were hardly any real thoughts behind it, just the two sides of her fighting things out blindly. She was back at the foster home, in the doorway to Ms. Clavens' office, her feet trying to figure out if they should take her into the room and toward her new foster home, or out onto the street and into that great void of uncertainty. She saw Ben's hands wrapped around hers, so tightly, and the questions in his eyes that only made more questions in her heart. "Ben, I stopped believing in things a long time ago. I stopped believing in dragons and princesses, knights in shining armor, and true love. But most of all I stopped believing in myself." She barely knew the words were out of her mouth until she was done, and she wished she could eat them back up before anybody could hear them. But she couldn't, and he did. He looked down at their hands, his brow wrinkled, and back up at her again. He leaned across the table and touched his lips to hers.

"I believe in you."

Eighteen

"The Wanderer is not alone, sir."

"What do you mean?"

"There is someone else with her on a frequent basis."

"And? Why do I care?"

"I'm fairly certain he knows about the dragon." Leonard wiped the beads of sweat from his upper lip.

"Another Wanderer? The Source? That's impossible."

"I don't think so, sir. There's no indication as such. I mean, I think he's a Believer."

"Hmph. I haven't seen any of those around in quite some time. I wasn't certain there were any still in existence."

"It would seem so, sir," Leonard replied. "Who else could it be?"

His master stared out the long window, saying nothing and scratching what was left of his scraggly beard. He finally turned to Leonard, a quietly menacing gleam in his eye. "Very well, then. If they want to increase the death toll, let it be on their shoulders."

Nineteen

Dragons are not a common part of human life on Earth. As a Wanderer, you have the rare opportunity for first-hand, one-on-one interaction. Most humans are not afforded this experience, or even the chance to believe in their existence. Bear this in mind as you raise your Dragonette.

Before you consider sharing the fact that you are a dragon's foster parent, think about the reactions you can expect from your fellow man. Many will not believe you, which is probably the lowest degree of adverse human reaction you could expect. As stated before, dragons as a part of reality are a bit beyond the capabilities of the collective human consciousness.

Be prepared for people to ridicule you, or even force you to undergo psychiatric evaluation. The latter must be avoided at all costs, as it can lead to institutionalization. This will leave your dragon to fend for itself until maturity, which is exceedingly dangerous. When this has happened in the past, it has proven incredibly difficult to get a new Wanderer to the Dragonette and take over his foster care. This also creates the problem of whether or not your Dragonette and the replacement Wanderer are able to bond.

That being said, it is natural for humans (Wanderers included) to want to share things with their fellow man. If you can find a Believer, feel free to let them into your world.

Aubrey's hand trembled as she tried to get the key in the lock. She didn't realize she could still be so nervous even while tipsy. The sober part of her brain was shaking its finger at her for letting Ben drive her home in the first place, which was not what she had originally planned on. *Hey, I shouldn't be driving anyway. What's a girl to do?*

"Aubrey, are you sure you're okay?" Ben asked again, as he watched her fumble with the keys. "If you're worried about the guy from the bar, I'm more than happy to come in with you for a bit. Not trying to be too forward or anything, just…"

"It's okay, Ben," she stopped him. "Hugo will protect me. I'll be alright." She smiled up at him, and he leaned in and kissed her gently.

"You know, I'd like to meet Hugo if I could. I love dogs."

She wanted to laugh, but he would probably question her sanity. Then a thought crossed her mind that she never would have imagined. "Ben, can I trust you?"

"Of course. Is everything okay?"

"Yes, I just…Well, you'll understand after I show you. He's not exactly an ordinary house pet." Her heart didn't pound in her chest so much as rattle around inside it like a rock in a tin can. Once they were inside and the door was shut and locked behind them, Aubrey made sure all the curtains were closed. During the day she didn't worry so much, but at night with the lights on she knew someone could easily see in as they drove by. The last thing she needed was the cops showing up with a report of an illegal wild animal or something. In her peripheral vision she could see Ben watching this routine with curiosity.

"He's in here." She opened the door to the kitchen and looked inside. At first she didn't see Hugo, just his empty plate and near-empty water bowl. She was going to have to find a better way to take care of him during the day.

"Over there." She stepped aside so Ben could see and pointed under the kitchen table, where Hugo was curled up in a scaly ball, fast asleep.

She turned to Ben to gauge his reaction. She knew that even though he was very into the fantasy of dragons, and her best bet for someone to share this with, there was still a chance it could be too much for him. The look of utter disbelief on his face made her wonder if this was a big mistake. She cringed, waiting for him to run screaming out the front door and take off as fast as his hybrid car would let him.

"Is that...um...oh, Aubrey!" She saw his eyes gloss over with tears, and instantly felt terrible. Half of her guilt was for upsetting Ben, and the other half was that she hadn't been in nearly that much awe when she first met Hugo.

She walked over to the table and pulled out one of the kitchen chairs so she could wake the sleeping dragon, thinking of the irony of what she was doing. As soon as he felt the chair move, Hugo was awake and bounded out from under the table. He rubbed his head on Aubrey's leg like a happy cat, then peered around her knee at Ben.

"Ben, I would like you to meet Hugo. Hugo, this is my friend Ben." Hugo looked up at her uncertainly before stalking across the kitchen to meet the new human. He fluttered his shiny wings and sniffed the air.

Ben was still standing in the kitchen doorway, mouth agape. He closed it, as though suddenly waking up from the shock of this new discovery. "Can I touch him?"

"Yes, I think so. I mean, I've never introduced him to anyone else before. The only real way to know is to try. If he decides he doesn't like you I imagine he'll let you know."

He kneeled down and stretched out a tentative hand. Hugo sniffed the proffered hand, then butted his head up underneath it.

Aubrey laughed, shattering the tense silence. "I think he wants you to pet him."

Ben obliged as much out of his own desire as Hugo's demands. "This is absolutely incredible," he said, finding his tongue again. "I have so many questions for you I don't even know where to start."

Twenty

The alarm reverberated through Aubrey's head, trying desperately to pull her back to consciousness. Every buzz reminded her of the few beers she'd had and how late she had stayed up. She and Ben had sat at the kitchen table until two in the morning, talking about Hugo. She told him everything. He already knew about the book, but not that it was real. She explained how the little dragon had come into her possession, and everything she had learned about him so far. Hugo seemed to enjoy the attention, and after a late dinner of flame-broiled chicken spent his time going back and forth between the two humans and getting as many pets and belly rubs as he could.

"I just don't understand," Ben had said. "I mean, it's something I would have given anything to see, and now that it is right here in front of me I just can't wrap my head around it. There is a *dragon* in your kitchen!"

"I know, it's crazy. But now you can see why I said my

life has changed so much in the last few days. Hugo has given me a lot to think about, and maybe that's a good thing right now, but I worry. What happens when he gets bigger? He's already grown a ton. Where will I keep him? What if someone finds out about him? Sometimes I think the old man at the carnival gave the box to the wrong person."

"Don't be so down on yourself. I'm sure he knew what he was doing."

"But why not someone else? Why not someone like you?"

"And what, exactly, makes me more qualified?"

"Because you never let the fantasy go."

"Neither did you. I know you think you did, but what about your volunteer work at the library? You not only keep the fantasy alive, you spread it around for other people to enjoy. What I do on the weekends is just a little selfish entertainment compared to what you do. I think you are the perfect person for Hugo, and it's obvious that he thinks so, too." Right at that moment, Hugo was perched in Aubrey's lap and was rubbing his head on the bottom of her chin. "I think it's just one of those meant-to-be things, and it works out the way it's supposed to."

"Do you really believe that?"

"I believe in dragons, so why not? And what about how you got the book? Nobody gave that to you, at least not that you know of, so there must be something bigger going on here than just an old carnie picking a random customer. It's not like picking up a stray cat on the side of the road, although I'm sure someone would argue there's some predestination there, too. But anyway, that's not the point. This is deep stuff. At least you have the book to guide you."

"You would think that," Aubrey replied. "But a lot of it is

pretty vague. I've seen those books on baby care that tell you every single thing you could need to know about a newborn, but this isn't anything like that. I feel like I'm flying by the seat of my pants." By this time her buzz had worn off and she felt somber and tired, if not quite as lonely.

When they had finally decided to call it quits and realized what time it was, Aubrey invited Ben to stay. "Just cause, you know, it's really really late and I don't want to have to worry about you driving home." He had given her a sleepy, knowing smile and gratefully accepted the pillow and blanket she offered him.

Now, as she dragged herself out of bed, she wondered at the sensibility of her invitation. After all, they both had to go to work. Ben would still be in his clothes from the previous day, and her car would still be in the office parking lot. Anybody that got there before they did would instantly think they knew exactly what had happened. Despite her blooming feelings for Ben, she was not ready to deal with that kind of ridicule.

"Ben!" she called as she stumbled down the hall. Maybe if she could get Hugo taken care of, she could get dressed quickly enough that they could run to his place and at least get him into some different clothes before heading to the office. "Ben, are you up?" She came into the living room to find the couch empty, other than the folded-up blanket and pillow. "Ben?" *Surely he didn't skip out on me...*

She could hear a trilling noise coming from the kitchen, and opened the door. Ben was on the floor with a plate of fruit and a fork. Hugo was in his lap, eating the fruit off the fork as Ben offered it to him. "Good morning, sleepyhead. I hope we didn't wake you. I slept for a few hours, but I was just too excited. And someone here was ready for breakfast." He stabbed a strawberry and Hugo quickly freed the fork of it.

"Sleepyhead, yourself," she giggled. His dark hair was standing nearly straight up from his attempts at sleep. "You're going to have him spoiled."

"Spoiling a dragon? That sounds like the kind of opportunity I don't want to miss."

Since Hugo had eaten, Aubrey was able to get ready for work while Ben prepped the dragon food for the rest of the day. They scrambled out the door and to his apartment for a fresh change of clothes. She nearly declined when he invited her in, but since they'd already spent a whole night together it seemed silly. She sat in the living room and admired his medieval décor while he stepped into his bedroom to change. While he had a modern couch and a flat screen television, there were plenty of dragons and swords to castle it up a little bit.

"Hey, is this your coat of arms?" she called to him as she admired a hand painted shield on the wall. It was white with a black greyhound, and three gold coins across the top. 'Blackwell' had been carefully scripted across the center.

Ben emerged from the bedroom, buttoning his shirt. "Yeah, I made it in high school for part of an art project. It's not the nicest looking coat of arms out there, but it's mine."

"Wow, you made it yourself? I never would have guessed."

"I started getting into dragons and medieval stuff when I was in junior high. A lot of it had to do with this." He pulled a battered hardback copy of *The Once and Future King* off the bookshelf. "Not the kind of thing that gets you any looks from the girls, but I wasn't exactly popular anyway. It's hard to have a chance when you have your nose in a book all the time."

"It sounds like you and I would have gotten along just fine in high school."

When they got to the office parking lot, only Aubrey's car was there, and looked rather lonesome. Ben grabbed her elbow as she reached for the door handle.

"Aubrey, before you go, I really want to say what an incredible time I had last night. Not just because of the amazing mythical creature in your kitchen, either."

She smiled at him. "So did I." She kissed him quickly but gently, and was off to her cubicle.

Twenty-One

"The doctor will see you now, Miss Goodknight." The nurse led Aubrey back to the doctor's office. With the bedside manner he had, she was not expecting a personal meeting with him. The news must be terrible.

The body scan had gone about as she had imagined. The machine had clicked and whirred around her but she kept her eyes closed. She wasn't sure she could handle it if she had opened them. Her scared mind managed to wander all over the place, but mostly to Ben and Hugo. Was she really finding her dream guy right as she faced the possibility of death? And what about Hugo? She engaged her mind with awful fantasies about her orphaned dragon, taken in by Ben only to find that he wants to put the poor baby in the circus. At that thought she had to mentally slap her wrist. No matter how much he denied it, Ben was a far more qualified foster parent than she was.

Three days later she was here, sitting across a desk from

Dr. Crawford. Her stomach had clenched itself into a tiny ball of fear inside her. A file folder was in front of him, disturbingly thick with paperwork and bearing her name on the tab. He tapped his finger on the front of it.

"Aubrey, I have often gone over scan results over the phone with my patients, but in your case I felt I should talk to you in person."

Oh, God. Here's where he tells me I'm dying.

"As you know, we wanted to do the body scan to test for any cancer that may have spread to other parts of your body from the lump in your breast. This is a pretty standard thing we do. We want to know exactly what we are in for before we schedule any kind of treatment."

Why didn't I let Ben come with me for this? Or Betty? Somebody. She could feel sweat popping out on her forehead.

Dr. Crawford opened the file. "The good news is that the body scan didn't find any additional suspicious tissues." He paused for what seemed to Aubrey an infinite amount of time. She noticed that he looked a little pale, and the set of his mouth was so hard it was barely more than a line across his face. "The incredible news is that we couldn't find the original tumor, either."

Aubrey blinked at him a couple times. The doctor continued flipping through the file, as though he was trying to find the lump hidden between the pages.

"I hate to admit to you that I am really not certain what happened. I know from my own memory and the information in your file that the lump was there very recently. Hell, we did a biopsy on it." He took off his glasses and rubbed his hand over his face.

"I...I don't even know what to say." *I'm a freak.*

"Quite frankly, neither do I. I'm amazed. I have never seen or heard of a case like yours. Have you been doing anything special?"

The sweat was drying on her forehead now, and she just felt cold and tired. She knew she should be ecstatic, but she was more exhausted than anything. "Um, just eating a lot of organic foods, fresh produce." She thought of Hugo and his blue light. "That's about it."

"Well you must have eaten something right, then. I'd like you to come back in a month for a few more tests. I want to make sure everything is accurate here." He put his glasses back on. "And if it is, don't be surprised if the university gets in contact with you for a case study. You are one of a kind." As he showed her out of the office, she noticed the nurses giving her an odd look.

"Ben? It's me. I'm sorry to call you at work."

"Hey, beautiful. I don't mind. How did it go?"

She felt hot tears prickling her eyes. "It's...I...it's gone." The tears flooded over her lashes and down her cheeks. She could barely see her car in the parking lot as she dug in her purse for her keys. The ball of fear that her stomach had been was now a watery mass, drowning all the words she wanted to say to Ben in its deathly depths.

"Aubs, do you need me to come pick you up? Are you okay?"

She tried to take a deep breath and get herself together, but it just ended in a sob. "Oh, Ben. I think...I think I'm just going to go home and lay down. But it's gone." She was in her car now, trying to wipe the tears from her eyes so she could see the road, or even the steering wheel. "I think Hugo did it. The cancer is all gone. They couldn't find any of it."

For a moment, there was only silence on his end of the phone. "But that's great! We should celebrate! If you are *sure* you can get home okay, then why don't you go relax and I will bring over some champagne tonight when I get off."

Aubrey nodded to the phone. The alcohol might help the headache she was sure to get from crying so hard. "That would be nice."

"You call me if you need anything else, okay?"

"Okay."

Ben came as promised, but champagne wasn't the only thing he brought. When he showed up at the door she could barely see him behind the dozen pink roses he carried. He had also picked up dinner, which Aubrey was infinitely grateful for. The roses were great but she was too exhausted to cook. Ben laid out roast beef, green beans, mashed potatoes with gravy, and a huge chocolate cake for dessert. Hugo eagerly joined them for dinner but turned his silvery nose up at the chocolate cake. Ben listened intently as she explained Hugo's healing blue light, nodding between forkfuls of cake and glancing back and forth between her and the dragon. "Amazing."

That night after Ben left, Aubrey didn't close the door to the kitchen. She left it and her bedroom door open. Hugo curled up next to her, his head on the pillow and butted up right next to hers.

"Spoiled dragon."

Twenty-Two

Aubrey wrapped Hugo in an old blanket and hefted him out to the car. She put him in the passenger floorboard. "Now you stay down there, you hear me? I can't possibly be heading down the highway with a dragon sitting up in the passenger seat. There will be wrecks all along the road and we'll get an involuntary police escort, for sure."

The address that Ben had given her led them quite a ways out into the country, far from suburbia and even farther from industrial downtown. Ben's car was already there, the top half of him diving into the trunk.

"Who's up for a picnic?" he called as he pulled out a basket. "I figure if we want anything cooked we can let Hugo play chef."

"I'm not sure how much he can do yet, but we'll see." She opened the passenger door and lifted the blanket off of Hugo. He bounded out the door in a flash of sunlit silver and barreled towards Ben.

"Hey, little guy! Well, okay, not so little anymore!" he amended as Hugo butted his head into Ben's knees. "Let's go over this way," he said as he pointed to a trail leading into the woods. "It's pretty private out here anyway, but might as well not risk staying close to the road."

"So what exactly did you bring us here for? And who owns this place?" Aubrey asked as they headed away from the road and into the trees.

"Well, technically I do." Ben replied. "This land has been in my family for a long time. I think at one point there was an old house here, but nobody has lived here for ages."

"Do you think you would ever want to live here? I mean, instead of living in town in your apartment?"

"I don't know for sure. I've thought about it before, but it just never seemed like the right time. I've been doing some freelance IT work on the side, and if I could get that to take off enough to do it full time, then that might change things. I wouldn't have to worry about a commute, and I could spend my lunch breaks indulging in this beautiful scenery." He smiled at Aubrey. "But then again, I've found some awfully beautiful scenery in the break room, too."

She blushed and looked down at Hugo, who was not patient enough for their human pace nor their human discussion. He scampered circles around them, shaking his wings and sniffing every blade of grass.

"I'm glad that I can finally put it to at least some use, and let Hugo practice out here," Ben continued. "He's not going to get good practice at flying by hanging off your ceiling fan."

"How sweet of you. I think he appreciates it, too. Poor guy has never been out of my house until now. But, it seems like there are far too many trees here. I don't know that he'll have enough room to fly, at least not by the time he gets a little bigger."

"Just wait until we get to the top of this hill. You'll see. It's the perfect place for him."

Ben's promise held true. As they topped the hill, they broke through the trees and onto the rim of a huge valley. There were still a few clumps of trees scattered here and there but for the most part it was open field. In the very bowl of the valley sat a lake, clear blue as the sky and smooth as glass.

"It's beautiful, Ben! What do you think, Hugo?" She looked down where Hugo sat at her feet.

He shook his wings for the millionth time that day, then opened them fully with a dramatic snap. He let out a shrill howling sound, his baby version of a dragon's roar, and set his feet in motion. He flapped his wings as he built up speed down the hill and leapt into the air. The little dragon soared out over the lake, taking a full circle around it before returning to the ground.

Aubrey looked to Ben with tears in her eyes. "I'd say he likes it."

Hugo spent a good part of the morning practicing. He took off and landed countless times before Aubrey could bring herself to finally interrupt him. "Hugo! Let's break for lunch!" she called out to him. Obliging, he swooped back to his human. She and Ben had found a nice flat spot by the lake and were laying out the picnic Ben had packed.

"I tried to stick with stuff that I figured we would all like," Ben said as he opened the cooler. "Lots of fresh fruits and vegetables, some organic deli meat with whole wheat bread, and some chicken for Hugo, uncooked of course."

"I have to admit I probably would have gone off the

organic diet now that the cancer is gone, but Hugo has really helped keep me on it. That's not such a bad thing though. I know it's healthier, and I feel good, and my pants fit better."

"Your pants have always fit nicely, if you ask me."

Aubrey smirked at him. "Fresh."

"Just like the lunch. I did bring a treat for later though."

"What's that?"

"A surprise is what it is."

Hugo was trying to push open the top of the picnic basket with his nose, eager to see what Ben had brought. Ben set a paper plate of cut-up raw chicken in front of him. Hugo scooped up one of the pieces in his mouth and promptly spit it out. He glared at Ben and let out a hiss accompanied by a puff of smoke.

"Cook it yourself, then, lazy dragon." Ben stabbed one of the pieces with a fork (he had been sure to pack a few metal ones so they wouldn't melt) and held it in front of Hugo's snout. "Go on. Torch it."

Hugo studied Ben for a moment, blinking his eyes and giving a few snorts toward the chicken. Aubrey wondered for the first time if Hugo could understand Ben as well as he could understand her. She soon found out. The dragon pulled his head back and puffed out his chest. As his head shot forward toward the chicken, he opened his mouth. Aubrey tensed, waiting for the fireball. The resulting flame, though, was only equivalent to a few matches. It singed the side of the chicken closest to him.

"Good try, Hugo!" Aubrey tried to stroke his head but he shook her off. This time he arched his head so far back that it was almost over his wings. He shot forward again and aimed for the chicken. A flame like a blowtorch came out between his fangs, cooking the chicken the rest of the way.

"Yeow!" Ben screeched as he dropped the burning hot fork, chicken and all. "I guess I should have thought that through a little better. Next time I'm bringing oven mitts." The dragon ignored him and plucked the piece of chicken off the fork, gulping it down happily.

"I just can't believe it," said Aubrey. "He's getting too big too fast."

"You sound like such a mom."

"Well, I kinda am."

The smile dropped from his face. "Yeah, I guess that's true. But what are you going to do with him? I mean, eventually he's going to get too big for your house, much less your car."

She shrugged. "We don't know that for sure, do we? This is the first dragon either one of us has ever seen, after all. Maybe they get to be about the size of a German shepherd and then they stop."

"I'd like to agree with you on that."

"But you don't."

"No. I'm sorry. But we'll figure it out. Don't worry."

"I always worry. That's what moms do, right?"

When the light began to fade, Ben wouldn't listen to Aubrey's suggestion to pack up. "You didn't even get your treat yet." He set up a campfire and invited Hugo to light it for him. It took a couple of tries, but he soon had a nice blaze going. Then Ben unpacked graham crackers, chocolate bars, and a big bag of marshmallows. "I figured if we were going to be out here, we might as well have a little bit of fun."

Hugo seemed to enjoy toasting the marshmallows for them, despite the blazing campfire, but he refused to eat any of them. That was just as well for Aubrey, who couldn't remember the last time she had a s'more. Then she did remember something.

"It's Saturday!"

"I sure hope so," Ben replied. "Otherwise we are really late for work by now."

"No, I mean wasn't LARP today?"

"Technically, yes. But it was too hard to convince myself to go when I have something so much better here. After all, I've never been to a LARP event that featured a real live dragon *and* a beautiful princess."

"And how will the kingdom fare without King Arthur?"

"I like to think they will manage."

Twenty-Three

"He's nearly ready, sir."

"Are you sure? I don't want any more incidents out of you."

Leonard nodded, and this time even Max backed him up. "It's true, sir. I saw him myself, and he will be crossing over any day now."

"You are confident he is old enough to make the transition? It takes a lot of power to open a wormhole like that."

Leonard looked to Max. Even he had little beads of sweat popping out on his forehead. "I cannot be sure of the exact date, but I know it will be soon. He's young still, but he's a silver. He's powerful. And recent records show they've been crossing over at consistently younger ages."

"Very well. Increase your patrol and be on your feet. Make sure someone notifies me as soon as the dragon makes his move. One tiny swirl of the time-space continuum and I had better be notified."

Twenty-Four

A Warning to Wanderers

You have no doubt at this point had some thoughts about how difficult it is to raise a dragon. This would be a very correct notion, indeed, considering that dragons do not belong in your world. Even so, the most difficult and dangerous part of your journey is yet ahead of you.

Once your Dragonette has mastered his basic life skills, it is time for him to go home. Most Wanderers have mixed feelings about this, as they have become attached to their foster child and yet they are ready for a break. Do not despair at the thought of missing your Dragonette. Once a Wanderer, always a Wanderer. You will have opportunities to visit with your dragon frequently.

There are those who seek to find your dragon's home, and so the journey could be quite hazardous for the both of you. Take all precautions necessary.

Aubrey stood on the rim of the valley, right where she was when she had first seen it. She and Ben had spent a lot of time here over the last few months. Hugo was the size of a horse now, and she couldn't keep him at home. She had tried for as long as she could, but when she came home to find his scaly rump pressed against the picture window, she knew it was time to do something. Ben had helped her build a shelter for him down by the lake, and she visited him every day. They had camped out a few nights when they could take advantage of the weather, and even if it was chilly it was no problem for Hugo to light a fire for them at this point.

And that, sadly, was why they were here. Ben stood next to her and laced his fingers through hers. It's just as hard for him, she thought. Hugo stood on the other side of her, and after a last long look at the valley nuzzled his head against her. He nearly knocked her down but she didn't mind. He gave Ben the same treatment and then spread his wings.

Aubrey tried to wipe the tears out of her eyes so that she would be able to see his final takeoff. The sun glinted sharply off his now-huge wingspan as he headed out over the lake. Just like that first day, he took a full circuit of the water. But this time he didn't fly back to them. He soared on, past the lake, past the other side of the valley, past where the trees started back up again. The dragon rose higher and higher and disappeared into the clouds. She couldn't hold the tears back any longer. She sank to her knees, closing her eyes against it all.

"Aubrey." She kept her eyes shut. Not even Ben's voice or his arms around her could make the gaping hole in her heart feel better. "Aubrey, don't cry. It's just a dream." But she didn't want Hugo to be a dream. Even if he had to leave her, she wanted, needed, him to be real.

Sobbing, she opened her eyes to find that she was not in the valley after all. She was at home, in her bed. The morning sun blazed in through the gap in the curtains, mimicking the glare off the lake and Hugo's wings. "Oh, Ben, it was terrible. I dreamed about Hugo going home. To Parandour."

Ben sighed and pulled her closer into his arms. "I wish we knew more. The guidebook is so ambiguous about everything. That doesn't make it very easy."

"No," Aubrey agreed. "I don't like it when I don't know what's expected of me. It says I have to guide him home, but just what the heck does that mean, anyway? It's not like I can just pull up a map online and send him on his merry way." She buried her face in the pillow. "And even though I don't know exactly when this is going to happen, I do know I'm running out of time."

"I'm sorry, sweets."

"No, I'm sorry." She turned so she could see Ben's face better and swiped at the tears spilling over her lashes. He had come into her life a few months ago, just as everything was turned upside down. It seemed like he had set it all right again. Not for the first time, she marveled at how things had changed for her. Having a dragon was not the kind of lifestyle she could share with just anyone, and she was terrified she would drive him away. "I had no idea I could get so emotionally wrapped up in a dragon. I hope you don't think I'm too much of a freak."

"A freak? Well, let's see. I had a massive crush on you from the first day I saw you in the break room. You introduced me to not only my first dragon but my first mythical creature. You are beautiful and sweet and treat this foster child as though he was your own. If that is a freak, then I like freaky."

Aubrey involuntarily smiled through her tears and cuddled in closer to Ben. "Where have you been all my life?"

"Oh, you know, just dressing up in chainmail, waiting for my princess to come."

"Everything is so different than it was just a few months ago. I've had and gotten rid of cancer. I've become a foster parent. My perception of reality has completely changed. And," she wrapped her hand around his, "I found my Prince Charming. Or King Arthur, as the case may be. I love my life, but sometimes I feel like if I blink it will all go away, and be just like it was before. Before Hugo. Before you."

"That won't happen."

"It happened before."

"I won't let it." He wrapped his arms even tighter around her. "I know you don't like change, but..."

"No, I don't!" Aubrey cringed as she heard the snap in her voice. "I'm sorry."

Ben paused for a moment, and Aubrey tensed in the silence. He sighed. "Sometimes change can be good though, right?"

She closed her eyes and concentrated on the heat that emanated from his body, the force he created as he wrapped himself around her. "Yes." But she wasn't sure she believed it.

"Why don't we go ahead out there to see him? Maybe that will make you feel better."

"Okay," she sniffled.

When they got to the valley, Hugo was nowhere in sight. Aubrey's stomach twisted with worry.

"I'm sure he's just off hunting or something." Sure enough, the sun was soon blocked out for a moment as Hugo sailed above them, screeching devilishly. He landed with a thud and before he had even folded his wings he was rubbing his head on Aubrey's shoulder. She didn't know if he was trying to be affectionate or if he had an itch, but she really didn't care. Then she noticed that his wings were still opened partway.

"What is it, baby? Are you hurt?" She had often chastised herself for talking to this dragon like a human toddler, but since he didn't seem to mind she told herself that she didn't either. After all, she had hatched him from an egg. She tried to look him over for an injury, but he was moving too much. He danced from foot to foot, shook his wings, and screeched some more.

"I've never seen him act like this before."

"I don't suppose there's anything in the book about it, is there?" Ben asked.

"I've read that thing from cover to cover and back again, and nothing comes to mind. He seems really upset." Aubrey tried to stroke his head but he was still dancing too much for her to get close without getting knocked over.

Suddenly, Hugo went still. He looked up into the sky and let out that shrill screech again. The sun was blacked out once again but this time the shadow they were under was much bigger than when Hugo had passed over them. Aubrey looked up to see what seemed like endless shimmering scales.

Twenty-Five

"It is nearly time, then, isn't it?"

"Yes, sir. I certainly hope so, sir," Leonard replied.

The robed figure looked up from the heavy tome in front of him and fixed his pale eyes on Leonard. "I wonder sometimes why you are so interested. I wonder if, perhaps, you are a bit too interested."

"N-no, sir," Leonard stammered. "I just want to go to Parandour, sir. To help you reclaim what is rightfully yours."

"Mmm, indeed. It has been far too long since I have been home." He cast the hood of his robe back, angling his face towards the candlelight. "Tell me, Leonard. What do you see? The face of a great and powerful wizard? Or merely a decrepit old man, lacking what he needs most to sustain his form and strength?"

Leonard cringed as he looked upon his master. Where there might have been a grizzled gray beard, only random strands of scraggly hair poked out of his flaccid chin. One eye had gone completely cloudy, and though Troninn had never mentioned it, Leonard was fairly certain he couldn't see with it anymore. Craters and pits bombed the rubbery skin of his face. "Surely, ah, surely the face of a great and powerful wizard, sir." He struggled to keep the question out of his voice.

"Liar!" Troninn boomed, pointing a yellowed fingernail at Leonard. "There is nothing for us here in this world! Only deceit and decay! Oh, but just you wait." His voice had lowered again. "I will soon turn the tables. It will be the dragons who can no longer thrive, with only Earth magic to live on. We'll see how well they do when they are deprived of the magic of Parandour!"

"Yes, sir. Indeed, sir."

"You sniveling sheep! You disgust me! Consider yourself lucky that I need you too badly to kill you right now."

"Yes, sir. My apologies, sir." He stared at his feet for a moment, trying not to look at Troninn's disfigured face, but not wanting him to notice he wasn't looking. "What would you have me do, sir?"

"The Dragonette is nearly grown. The Wanderer will be crossing him over soon. Following them isn't going to be enough. If they decide to open the portal and I'm not there, it could be too late. I want you to capture the Wanderer."

Leonard had to keep his jaw from dropping. "And, begging your pardon, sir, but what then? Won't the Dragonette need her to make the transition?"

"Certainly he will. And also most certainly, the Dragonette won't leave her side. Our victory will be all the sweeter if they have contributed to each other's deaths and don't even know it. Tell the others to be prepared. I have a feeling she's going to put up a bigger fight than the last one."

Twenty-Six

"Um, I think we have a visitor," Ben said.

"I just hope it's on friendly terms with us." Aubrey looked away from the gigantic dragon above her and back toward Hugo, hoping to gauge the situation by his reaction. He continued to hop and dance about, rattling his wings and screeching. She couldn't tell if he was excited or terrified, and she felt much the same way.

She had told Ben the truth when she said she had read the whole book. It had directed her not to read ahead, and she hadn't. But Hugo had mastered it all by now. The last chapter had talked about taking Hugo to Parandour, and she knew that would be coming soon. It never said anything about other dragons coming back to Earth.

Hugo took to the air and flew circles around the new dragon as it sought a landing spot in the valley. The silver dragon was still quite nimble despite his increasing size, and had no problem landing just about anyplace he wanted. The larger dragon, however, seemed to be trying to find a spot big enough to house its entire frame. It finally settled down by the lake and Hugo shot to the ground next to it.

"What do you think we should do?" she asked Ben.

"I guess the only thing we can do is go down there. If it isn't friendly, it won't matter how close we are or how fast we can run."

They headed down the slope toward the dragon. *No, dragons,* Aubrey corrected herself. Going from one dragon suddenly to two felt like double vision, except the new dragon was an iridescent purple, and at least three times the size of Hugo. Just one of its wings was easily as long as a bus. As she got closer, Aubrey could see that even the talons on this beast were immense. It made a grumbly purring noise at Hugo as he rubbed his head against any part of it that he could reach. For the first time in a while, Hugo actually looked small.

The new dragon turned its head to the humans as they approached. Aubrey could see that it had the same catlike eyes as Hugo, only much, much larger. Their deep gold contrasted beautifully with the dragon's dark violet scales. "Greetings, Wanderer," it said.

Aubrey stopped in her tracks. All those fantasy book she had read when she was younger were coming to life before her eyes. While she had read in the guidebook that Hugo would someday be able to talk to her, she had yet to see any signs of him trying. He gave every indication of understanding what she said to him, and that had seemed enough. Now there was a gigantic dragon, standing next to her dragon, talking to her. *This is even more unreal than my dream.*

"I am forever in your gratitude," the dragon said. The voice was deep and rumbly, like you would expect a dragon voice to be, but Aubrey thought it was distinctly feminine.

"And...and why is that?" she asked.

"Forgive me, I did not introduce myself. My name is Driel, or at least that is the best translation. You already know my son, whom I understand you have named Hugo." Driel gestured with a clawed hand toward the silvery dragon, who was happily nipping at her wingtips.

Aubrey gaped at her for a moment. She had read once about a woman who adopted a baby, only to have the birth mother show up five years later and try to claim the child. The article hadn't seemed all that interesting until now. "Yes, I...um...Is that okay? The name I mean?"

Driel gave a rumble that Audrey hoped was a laugh. "Of course. That is your choice, and he is happy with it. Dragons are not as worried about these things as you humans are. But speaking of names, what is yours, Wanderer?"

"I'm Aubrey, and this is Ben."

Driel seemed to study Ben for a moment, then turned back to Aubrey. "I hope you will forgive me for my intrusion to your world, but there is trouble afoot."

Twenty-Seven

Hugo very obligingly lit a campfire to fight against the coolness of the day, and probably even more so to show off to his mother. Driel herself gave off just as much heat as the fire did. The young dragon shook his wings proudly as he marched back to her side and curled up in a silver ball under her wing.

"You know," Ben said, "I'm kinda glad I got to meet the little dragon before the big dragon. As impressive as Hugo was, I think I would have peed myself if I met you first, Driel."

"I hope your friendship with Hugo has left you a bit drier than that," Driel rumbled. "I have to say, though, I'm quite surprised to find you here, Ben Blackwell."

"Me?" Ben nearly squeaked the word out, caught under Driel's scrutiny.

"Mmmm…indeed. Of course I knew there was a Wanderer here, but a Believer, too? That's a bit much for a dragon to take in."

"What do you mean?" Aubrey asked.

The great dragon shook her head, looking oddly human for a moment. "The last time a Believer was so involved in raising a Dragonette...well...Perhaps I should start at the beginning." She settled herself a little more into the grass and wrapped her tail around Hugo. "In the beginning, there was only Parandour. All creatures lived together for the most part in peace. The human leaders would employ either dragons or wizards to supply the magic for their reign. Kings needed magicians for healing and for visions. Initially there were no ill feelings by a dragon toward a king who decided to use a wizard, nor by a wizard for a king who chose to hire a dragon.

"One wizard came to power on the Wizard's Counsel that would change all of that. Rugorin argued that all men should use wizard power, and that the wizards should wage war on the dragons. He meant to obliterate the competition, and ensure that he and his brothers would always be needed.

"Many on the Wizard's Counsel scoffed at Rugorin, but there were enough greedy hearts present that eventually Rugorin became their Master. He led the wizards in a great battle against the dragons, and they had no choice but to follow him.

"One wizard was not so convinced. He was part human, and many believe that is what kept his heart pure enough to stand against Rugorin. He alerted the dragons and fought at their side against the wizards. His name has long been lost to time, but he is known as The First Believer."

"All this time I thought when the book said I was a Believer it just meant I didn't put Aubrey in a psych ward for telling me about her pet dragon," Ben marveled.

"Of course the wizards were furious at his betrayal and fought even harder against the dragons. The First Believer united his magic with that of the dragons to cast a spell that would bind the wizards forever. Unfortunately, Rugorin's counter spell backfired on all of them. The opposing spells created a rip in the space-time continuum, and Parandour was shattered into two worlds, creating Earth.

"The hapless humans, who were only just beginning to understand what was happening between the two magic forces, were sucked through the wormhole along with the wizards, leaving only dragons in Parandour."

Aubrey thought she could see a tear forming in the corner of Driel's eye. "But wasn't that a good thing for the dragons? They could do as they pleased, right?"

Driel blinked. "It would seem that way, but what were they to do without their humans? I know the stories on Earth are of fire-breathing beasts being slaughtered by 'brave' knights, but that's not how it actually works. We love our human companions, and we need their magic. It got pulled through the wormhole to Earth along with them."

Aubrey impatiently ran her fingers through her hair. "But we don't have any magic! How could you possibly need us?"

"You really need to ask me that? After I left the raising of my son to you, without so much as a question? Humans have the kind of magic that's needed for our Dragonettes to thrive. Your magic of love, and loyalty, and blind faith makes all the difference in the universe. Unfortunately, with no humans left on Parandour there was no way for us to do it on our own. We had to find a way to get our eggs to Earth."

"But why not just come yourselves?" Ben asked. "Obviously you can go back and forth between worlds."

"It's too risky. Only a motion of the counsel is what is allowing me to be here with you right now. Wizards abound in this world, and frightened humans, too. If something happened to us on Earth, there would be nothing for our children to go back to in Parandour. We have to have a Source to bring the egg to Earth, and a Wanderer to bring the Dragonette back."

"I don't get this Wanderer business," Aubrey said. "Now both you and the book have called me that. I don't even like to travel."

Driel turned her giant head to face Aubrey and aimed one critical catlike eye at her. She gave a low rumble that Aubrey thought was her version of a chuckle. "That doesn't have anything to do with it, child. If you were not a Wanderer, you would not be here."

Aubrey sat in uncomfortable silence, unsure of what to say.

"Do you remember when you become a Wanderer?" Driel asked. "It was many human years ago, though it may as well have been yesterday in dragon years. I can tell it is still very clear in your mind, too."

Aubrey was startled for a moment. She hadn't realized Driel was inside her head.

"You were with your birth parents when they died, yes?"

Images of that day flooded Aubrey's vision. One moment everything was normal, and the next moment complete chaos. *Seems a lot like how my life has been recently, too,* she thought. She tried to blink back the tears that were fighting to spill over her eyelashes, and she couldn't help but glare at Driel. "I've tried very hard not to think about that day. And I would still rather not." She choked back a sob. She hadn't yet told Ben all the details about the events of her childhood, but he saw her face and moved to wrap his arm around her waist. She let him.

"I'm afraid it is very important, painful though it may be. That was the day you lost your true tie to Earth. That day is why you are a Wanderer."

Now it was Aubrey's turn to give Driel a critical look. "So you're telling me every orphan is a Wanderer?"

"Every Wanderer is an orphan, but not every orphan is a Wanderer. Tell me, how were those explosions explained? Who was blamed?"

"Um, they said they were terrorists of some sort, I think," Aubrey stuttered. "Crime bosses were angry with the city government for ramping up their fight against them."

"And did they catch them?"

"No," Aubrey said. She couldn't say any more than that. She had spent the next several years of her childhood fearing another attack, knowing the bad guys were still out there somewhere. She never said anything to her adoptive parents, but looking back on it she thought they had known. Every time she had asked her new dad to make sure there was nobody outside her bedroom window or hiding in the closet, he had obliged without question.

Driel sighed, bringing Aubrey back to the present moment. "Humans tend to draw conclusions that satisfy their view of reality. They don't like to think of any other possibilities."

"What are you telling me?"

"I'm telling you that what humans may have called terrorists were in fact wizards. The same ones I told you about earlier."

"They were there to kill my parents?"

"They had no idea of the Wanderer they would make that day. They were there for a different Wanderer. They got him, and your parents, but we got you."

"Wizards kill Wanderers?"

"When they can, yes."

"Are they going to kill me?"

"They will try."

Twenty-Eight

By the time they left the valley, it was well past dark and Aubrey's normal bedtime.

"Do you want to stay at my place this time?" Ben asked. "It'll be a little closer for us for tonight, and I'm guessing we'll be going back to the valley tomorrow."

Aubrey nodded sleepily from the passenger seat. "Yeah, that's fine. My place feels too empty without Hugo staying there anymore, anyway." She turned to look at Ben, admiring the curve of his cheekbones in the oncoming headlights. "I hope Driel thinks I did an okay job with him."

Ben took his eyes off the road for a moment to glance at her. "What? With Hugo? Of course you did a good job. Doing, actually. You aren't done yet, remember?"

"Says you. You aren't a dragon mama."

"I'm pretty sure she would let you know if she wasn't happy with you. Even Hugo. He might be a quarter of his mother's size, but he could turn either one of us into barbecue if he wanted to."

Aubrey laughed softly. "Despite him being a dragon, it's hard for me to imagine him doing anything mean." They rode through the night in silence for a few minutes. "It's like we're living in a fairytale, Ben."

He smiled. "It's nice, isn't it?"

"Other than the part about wizards that want to kill me, yeah. But I feel like I'm just waiting to wake up. Like it can't actually be happening. After today, I feel like I should give Hugo back to Driel, not that I could stop her if she wanted him anyway, and just go back to my normal boring life. "

Ben pulled into his driveway and put the car in park, but instead of shutting it off he turned to look at Aubrey. "After all this time, you still don't believe? Aubs, you have been raising a dragon, you have met his mother, and you're going to help him cross over into a whole other world soon. You know though, I don't think that's the problem. It's not that you don't believe in what you're seeing with your own eyes, it's what you can't see that you don't believe in."

"What do you mean?"

"It's you. You don't believe in yourself. You don't believe that you can do this."

Aubrey held her head in her hands and pressed against her eyelids. "No, Ben. I really don't."

"But why not? Two dragons think you can do it. I think you can do it," he said softly.

Aubrey just shrugged and shook her head. "It just can't be me."

"And who exactly can it be?" he asked.

"Heck, I don't know. Maybe you. Maybe nobody. I just

don't think I can handle this. Any of it."

"What's that supposed to mean? Why are you acting like this?"

"Acting like what? Like I'm exhausted? Like I've been pushed beyond my mental and physical limit over the last several months? Well it's no surprise if I'm a little cranky, and I thought out of all people you would be the one to understand." She crossed her arms and turned her face toward the window, trying to hide her tears.

"Hey, now, wait a minute. I most certainly do understand if you're at the end of your rope, but that doesn't mean you should take it out on me." He tried to pull her hand toward him, but she snapped it back to her chest.

"Don't touch me, Ben Blackwell. Just take me home."

Twenty-Nine

"You understand the plan?"

"Yes, sir." The map of the city sprawled out on Troninn's desk was decorated with several push pins and uncountable numbers of marker lines. They had planned, re-planned, and re-planned again.

"And you are certain you can do the spell?" Troninn glowered at Leonard with a frightening countenance. "With Earth's limited magic, we have absolutely no room for error. If the mother dragon is here then surely they are onto us."

Leonard bit his lower lip, and just as quickly released it in case Troninn was watching. He fought the urge to wipe the beads of sweat off his forehead. "Forgive me for asking, sir, but wouldn't it be easier to move on the house? The Wanderer lives in a pretty quiet part of town."

"You dare to question me?" Troninn's spittle flew across the map as he screamed. "Don't you think I have examined this from every angle? Of course I know she lives in a quiet part of town. We've had her under close surveillance for months!" He drew his curved dagger from its place in his belt and held the point at Leonard's throat. "Question me again and you will find yourself on the wrong end of my magic. Now go get Max."

Thirty

The numbers on the screen were starting to blur. Aubrey rubbed her eyes and sighed. She hadn't worked late since Hugo showed up. She was always too eager to get home to him, knowing he was waiting on her. She would imagine him there in her kitchen, all alone and wondering if she really was going to return. Now that he was living out on Ben's acreage, she worried less, but only a little. He could hunt a little bit of food for himself, and stretch his wings all that he pleased, but he was still alone. At least, he had been until Driel showed up. Aubrey was glad he had company now, even if it couldn't be her. *It doesn't matter anyway. I'm going tomorrow to tell Driel she can take over raising Hugo.*

Giving up, she flicked off her screen and straightened her desk. She could review the report in the morning when her mind was fresh, and hoped it would be up to Mr. Milner's expectations. She just wasn't able to throw herself into it like she used to. Hugo had given her something else to focus on other than what was probably a dead end job, and she wasn't sure she cared anymore about ever getting that promotion she'd always wanted. Everything was dull and normal now, less than normal. *Dismal.*

"And now I'll go home to my dismal empty apartment, all alone, and cry myself to sleep thinking about Ben," she muttered to the empty elevator and pushed the button for the ground floor, her mind wandering to Ben and to Hugo. She had gone from being completely alone, to having her life completely full, and was about to go right back again. Just yesterday she'd allowed herself visions of a beautiful wedding with dragons in attendance, and Hugo presenting the rings with his huge talons. She wanted to laugh at herself, but the hard little ball in her stomach felt like it could just as easily make tears as laughs. Her sigh echoed on the elevator walls as it slowed down. "Just lovely. Way to go, Aubrey."

Crossing through the lobby, she dug her keys out of her purse. Maybe she could swing through a drive thru on the way home. It felt like ages since she'd devoured a burger and fries. She looked up from her purse and out towards her car as she headed out the door. It was the only car left in the parking lot, but she was not the only person. A figure in black leaned against the trunk of her car, the ember of his cigarette visible in the darkness.

Backing into the lobby, Aubrey ran for the stairs. She fumbled with the keys on her phone.

"Police department, how can I help you?" came a bored voice from the other end.

"Yes, I need help. There's…" *What? A wizard after me? They'll send the men in white coats instead of cop cars.* "Um, nothing. Nevermind."

"Ma'am?"

But she punched the end button and cut him off, frantically redialing her phone.

"Hello?"

"Ben, listen to me," she whispered. "There's someone in the parking lot by my car. I think they've found me. I don't know what to do."

"The parking lot? You're still at work?"

Aubrey turned the corner of the stairwell to head up the next flight. "I'm going back to my office. I don't know what else to do. I started to call the cops, but they're not going to believe me."

She could hear Ben's sigh, and the dinging of his car as he put the key in the ignition. "If it really is them, the police aren't going to be able to help us, even if they did believe you. I'll be there as soon as I can."

"Okay. I'm going up to my office, but we need Driel."

"It takes too long to get to her, and I'm not leaving you there alone. I'm going to get you out of there, and then we'll get the dragons."

"Okay," Aubrey breathed. She had reached her floor and was nearly to her cubicle when she felt the crackle in the air. Like the feeling right before lightning strikes, it made her palms and the soles of her feet tingle. It was coming from what she had thought would be the safety of her cubicle. There was someone in her chair.

"What's wrong?" she heard Ben ask as the phone slipped out of her hand. Slowly, her chair turned around.

"Aubrey," a voice rasped. "It's so nice to finally meet you. I am Troninn, descendant of Rugorin the Great." He wore a hooded robe, but Aubrey could see the pocked face and glittering eyes that stared out of the shadows at her. "I believe you have something that I'm interested in. Cooperate with me, and your fate might not be quite as bad."

Her blood pounded so hard in her skull she thought she would pass out. Aubrey slowly backed away from her cubicle. Can you run away from a wizard? "I...I don't have anything to give you," she stammered as she continued to back up, right into the arms of another robed wizard. He held her tightly as she struggled against him, her purse falling to the floor.

"This is my associate, Max. He already knows you quite well."

"Hey boss, can I keep her?" Max asked. He tightened his grip on Aubrey and ran his tongue up her cheek. Aubrey screamed as she tried to squirm away from him.

"Once we have the dragon I don't care what you do with her," Troninn spat.

Up! This was not from the wizard or the slimeball. Aubrey glanced frantically around the office, looking for the person she had missed. *Up!* The voice screeched again, rattling inside her head, piercing her eardrums from the inside.

Summoning every scrap of courage she could find, Aubrey raised her heeled boot and stomped as hard as she could on Max's instep. She pushed herself up as he doubled over, slamming him in the chin with the top of her head. He let go, and she stumbled for the stairs, dizzy from the impact.

"Silly mortal human," she heard Troninn's voice behind her. She flew up the stairs, her adrenaline carrying her more than anything. "You don't really think you can outrun me do you?" Glancing back over her shoulder, she could see the wizard floating up the stairs behind her, his feet invisible under his robes, the hem of which did not touch the floor.

Up! The voice was desperate. *Up! Up! Up!*

The last flight of stairs ended with the door to the roof, and Aubrey burst out into the crisp night. The roof was deserted. *Okay, I'm up. I'm as up as up can get. Now what?*

Troninn glided out the door and toward her. "You see, there isn't any getting away from me. I could have captured you months ago. I know where you live and work. I know about Ben. I most certainly know about Hugo. I even know about his mother. I have been waiting for the right time, and that is now. You are going to take me to Parandour."

"I don't know how to do that!"

"Oh," Troninn breathed, "I think you'll figure it out." The tips of his long jagged nails glowed green and crackled with energy. "If you don't, I'm sure I can find a way to persuade you."

Edge! Edge! Jump! Jump!

"No." She tried to sound firm but knew she was failing as she backed toward the edge of the roof. The heel of her boot slipped over the edge and she threw out her arms for balance.

"And just what makes you think you can win this?" the old wizard hissed. "What makes you think you're stronger than a powerful wizard such as I?"

Jump! Jump! Now! Now! The voice pounded in her brain.

"Because I believe." She stepped off.

Thirty-One

When it is time to guide your dragon home, the most important thing is to believe in him, believe in yourself, and let your magic work.

For a few seconds, there was nothing. For a few seconds, she was simply falling, the night air rushing past her ears. If someone had asked her what she thought would run through her head as she fell off a building, she would have imagined at least an "Oh shit." But there was nothing.

Then the whump as she hit dragon flesh. She grappled for one of the ridge-like scales that ran down his back. "Thank you, Hugo."

Hold on.

He swooped around the corner of the building and toward the parking lot. Pushing her hair out of her eyes, Aubrey could see that her car had now been joined by Ben's. The man she had seen in the parking lot was still there, a ball of red fire crackling between his hands and illuminating a wicked grin as he walked slowly toward Ben.

"No!" Her voice was lost in the wind being whipped up by Hugo's wings. She could feel his body expand underneath her and his back arch, and he shot a massive fireball of his own that consumed the wizard as well as her car. A wing beat louder than Hugo's hit her ears, and she looked up to see Driel sweep in over them. She descended to the fiery scene below them and snatched Ben up in her talons just before the car exploded, sending bits of metal into the air beneath his feet.

"Ben! Are you okay?" Aubrey tried to look underneath the great purple belly.

"I think my eyebrows might be singed off, but other than that I think I'm okay."

"Let's go," Driel thundered. "We don't have any time left here."

"What about Troninn?" Aubrey asked, but she wasn't sure Driel could hear. "And go where?"

"I took care of him, at least for the moment. But that won't hold him for long." She gestured with her big head toward the office building as they shot past it. The rooftop was completely engulfed in flames. "And we are going to Parandour."

Tears sprang to Aubrey's eyes. "Do I at least have a moment to say goodbye to Hugo?"

"There is no need. You are going with us, Wanderer."

Aubrey blinked her eyes against the wind and the night. She watched the buildings and streets pass beneath them. The world around her suddenly focused into sharp definition. The scaley back underneath her and the wind swirling around her became clear-cut and unambiguous.

"Going with you? To Parandour?"

"Hugo still needs your magic. Your job as a Wanderer is not yet complete, Aubrey. But we must hurry. I don't know what kind of forces Troninn has been able to build up here. I'm sure there are many more of them than just the few at your office. Hugo is not truly ready to go home, but if we don't leave now it may be too late. That is the only reason I am here." Driel scanned the horizon. "I only hope we can cross back over before any of the wizards catch up with us."

The industrial scenery below them quickly faded into suburbs, and was soon enough swallowed up by trees and farm fields. She couldn't remember ever having gone this fast before.

Sorry, Aubrey.

"Sorry for what? You saved my life!"

Car. It broke Aubrey's heart to hear such a sad tone from her dragon.

"Don't worry about it. I have a much better mode of transportation now." She dared to let go with one hand and stoke his neck. "And I doubt I'll need a car in Parandour."

"We're almost back to the valley. We'll need to land and rearrange ourselves before we open the portal. Hugo won't be able to fly fast enough with you on his back."

"Good!" Ben called from underneath her. "No offense Driel but this isn't exactly a first class flight!"

Searching the trees, Aubrey couldn't tell where they were at all, and was grateful for Driel's sense of direction. She didn't recognize the valley until they were right above it and descending towards the lake. She tensed herself for a rough landing, but Hugo braced his wings like giant parachutes and dropped them gracefully to the grass. Driel set Ben down with a gentle thump before swooping around to land herself.

"Are you okay?" Ben asked.

"Me? You're the one that was nearly turned into charcoal," Aubrey replied as she wrapped her arms around his neck. He held her tightly, and as nice as it was to fly on Hugo's back, it still didn't quite beat the sensation this man gave her.

Sorry, she heard again in her head. She turned to Hugo, who looked just as sad as he sounded.

"It is not your fault, Hugo, so stop apologizing. I'm the one that needs to be doing that. I'm sorry, Ben."

"He can talk to you now?"

Aubrey smiled at Ben. "Apparently. And thank goodness he can, or I wouldn't be here."

"So….does this mean we're okay now?"

A great splash brought her attention back to Driel, who was swishing her head in the water of the lake and encouraging Hugo to do the same. "Save your mush for later. The hardest part of the journey is yet ahead of us, Wanderer. Drink if you need it, because the rest of this is on you and Hugo."

"Me?" Aubrey squeaked. "What am I supposed to do?"

"Why, open the portal of course."

Aubrey's insides turned to water. "How the hell am I supposed to do that? The book never said anything about it. Wouldn't I have to have some sort of magic?"

Driel cast a sidelong glance at her. "I've already told you that you do have magic. All humans do, but some have more than others. And, since you are a Wanderer, you have the magic to open the portal."

Lost, Aubrey looked to Ben but only saw excitement in his

eyes. "See? I said you were special, didn't I?" He kissed her forehead. "You can do this, Aubrey."

"The Believer plays his role well," the great dragon chuckled. "Come now, we must be on our way. The two of you will be riding with me."

Ben boosted Aubrey up onto the great purple back before climbing up himself and settling in front of her. She wrapped her arms around his waist and buried her face in his shoulder. "I think we're ready," he said.

"Good. Now just remember--" Driel was cut off by a great crack, as though a tree had been struck by lightning. She looked to her right, the opposite end of the valley from the one they had come in on, and Aubrey and Ben followed her gaze. The noise did, indeed, have something to do with a tree, for a giant oak was engulfed in green flames. There was another crack and the tree next to it burst into greenness. Driel spat out a harsh word in what Aubrey could only guess was draconian. Her leathery wings unfolded with a snap and the massive body lurched up and forward.

"What was that?" Ben called out to the great dragon, trying to be heard through the air that rushed past them as they picked up speed. They would be off the ground soon.

"That," said Driel, with a little less effort, "is exactly what I was hoping to avoid. That would be Troninn's men."

"How did they find us?" Aubrey shouted. They were in the air now, and Aubrey expected Driel to fly up toward the starry sky. Instead, she was staying about twenty feet off the ground. She looked around for Hugo, and found him flying pace with Driel, looking very resolute.

"We'll talk later! Right now, just hold on!"

Driel's wings pushed the air past them in great gusts as

they headed for the treeline. More thundery cracks came from behind them, landing closer each time. Reaching the edge of the trees, Driel dropped down to just a few feet from the ground. A wide path opened up in front of them, big enough to be a good-sized road except that it started in the middle of nowhere. Hugo had to fly behind them now. The trees made a dark green canopy overhead that blurred into a tunnel, only lit here and there by bursts of colored wizard fire. A tree to her right blazed into blue flames, and she looked back to check on Hugo. He was right on Driel's tail, his eyes squinted with determination.

Through his wings she could see something else. A green ball of flame flew at a distance behind them. Smaller balls of flame shot out at intervals, and Aubrey could see now that these were aimed right at them but Driel's speed made their aim inaccurate. The larger ball of flame was trying to keep up. More fireballs flew behind the green one, yellow, orange and red.

"Are you okay?" Ben asked over his shoulder.

"Not really! We're being followed!"

Ben looked back and Aubrey could see her terror reflected in his face. He saw Aubrey looking at him, and quickly turned away. "I think they're gaining on us!" he called to Driel.

This time, Aubrey could feel Driel's rumbley laugh more than she could hear it, but the dragon didn't say a word. She sped on through the forest, and Aubrey saw a clearing in the trees that opened up ahead of them. The path ended there and she couldn't see where it opened back up on the other side. *Oh my God, I'm going to die in a dragon accident.* She could feel more vibrations from the dragon, but it wasn't quite the same. Driel had her eyes shut.

"Driel! Open your eyes!"

"I don't need to see. You look," she replied, with what might have been a crease of a dragon brow. "It's time for you to open the portal!"

A sense of panic tightened Aubrey's chest. *We're going to fly into a tree and die because I don't know what to do.* She continued to stare at the trees ahead of them, hoping for some clue.

Believe, Hugo echoed in her head.

"What?"

Relax. Believe.

Aubrey's attempt at deep breaths only proved how shaky she was, but she did them nevertheless. She closed her eyes and conjured up what she thought a portal to a fantasy land would look like, all swirling light and darkness, like a black hole. She felt the tension run out of her body as she held onto the image, and she could feel Hugo's presence in her head even though he wasn't speaking. He hummed, though, like Driel did, a rumbling vibration that muffled all the other noises around them. She didn't need to open her eyes to know that Hugo's blue light was once again engulfing her body. Everything around her, the dragons, the trees, the fireballs, even Ben, dropped out of her awareness. She saw nothing but the spiraling light that led through the wormhole and sucked the wind in with it. A crackling energy raced through her body.

Look.

Obeying, Aubrey looked up ahead. As though the clearing were nothing more than a picture in a book, Aubrey could see it tearing away piece by piece. She squeezed her arms once again around Ben, and though she could hear an *oof* out of him he didn't complain. The clearing continued to rip apart, shredding the scene before her, until the only thing left of it was a swirling mass of leaves and darkness.

The energy ripping through her body was now a tingling sensation that consumed her. It flowed down her face, into her arms and to her hands, leaving white sparks flying from her fingertips when she took one hand off Ben to look at them. The tingle shot down her spine and through her legs. Ben was sparking, too, but she didn't have a chance to say anything to him about it. They flew into what was left of the clearing and straight through the wormhole, sparks and all. Aubrey let go of the vortex and felt it slam shut behind her.

Epilogue

Aubrey shut her eyes as they entered the vortex, partly because she was terrified and partly because of the swirling debris around them. She felt Earth slip away behind them with a deafening roar, and then for a moment there was nothing but hollow silence. Driel rumbled to herself again. Then the noise started up once more, and she guessed they must be coming out the other side of the wormhole. She waited, her eyes shut and her arms around Ben.

"Aubrey, look," she heard Ben say.

She opened her eyes and looked around her, finding a world disappointingly just like the one they had left. The only difference was the early morning sunlight pouring down on their backs like honey. She was about to ask what went wrong when Driel spoke up.

"Welcome to Parandour."

They were flying over countryside, with grass and trees and lakes. Had they still been on Earth they would have surely been off Ben's property by now, but this land could easily have been some neighboring acreage. Hugo swooped through the air next to his mother, looking satisfied.

"What about whoever was chasing us? Where did they go?" Aubrey asked, looking behind them and seeing nothing.

"You closed the portal before they got to us. No more questions now, Wanderer. There will be time to talk soon. We have someone we need to visit first."

Driel descended at the edge of a copse of trees, where a little hut stood. The only sign of life was a small campfire with a kettle hanging over it. The great dragon glided down to the ground in front of the hut, Hugo following swiftly.

As the humans dismounted, the door to the hut opened. Aubrey had not expected to meet another human here, and certainly not to recognize him. He smiled and waved at Driel like an old friend as he approached. Aubrey gasped.

"What's wrong?" Ben asked, ready to jump to her defense.

"That's the old man from the carnival! The one that gave me Hugo's egg."

Driel heard her and smiled. "Aubrey, you can now officially meet Richard, your Source."

"Nice to see you again, young lady," said the old man, tipping his wide-brimmed straw hat at her. "And I see you've got yourself a Believer, too." He nodded at Ben. "Come in, come in. I have food and drink for you. I'll bet you need it, too."

Seeing Aubrey's hesitation, Driel nodded to her. "Go on, Wanderer. Hugo and I will be out here waiting for you. Enjoy your time with Richard; he's quite entertaining. We will have plenty of time to talk later."

Aubrey and Ben ducked under the low lintel behind the old

man. The inside of the hut was surprisingly spacious, but the furnishings were simple and sparse. A low bed slunk along one wall, with a short bookshelf serving as a nightstand. A table and chairs rounded out the ensemble, leaving most of the floor space empty. The ceiling, however, was bountifully hung with drying herbs, beans and peas, and sausages. Candles in metal lamps swung between them. "Please, sit." Richard gestured at the table and began to pour what looked like wine into ceramic mugs. Aubrey sat, out of exhaustion and confusion more than politeness. "I don't get to visit with other humans very often," he went on. He seemed to have left his churlish air back on Earth, and his beard now wiggled with enthusiasm as he spoke. "Not that the dragonfolk make bad company, mind you, but they certainly don't fit through a door, and you can't really cook for them." He cut down one of the sausages and produced a cheese from a cabinet, and began slicing it for them.

Aubrey's mouth began to water at the pungent scent of the food. It was simple fare, but she was used to that by now. "So, what's next?" she asked. "I mean, we got Hugo here, so…"

The old man chuckled. "That you did, missy. That you did. And just by a hair's breadth, I'd say. Driel's bound to be delighted with you. She was worried sick over that little one. If I ever saw a dragon wringing her talons it was her. But I knew he was in the right hands. And you," he pointed his knife at Ben, "were quite the help yourself. Don't think that won't go down in the history books. A Wanderer and a Believer, teaming up to defeat the wizards on Earth. It sounds more like a campfire story than the latest news." He shook his head, his beard swinging wildly. "All's well that ends well, eh? I've got your cottage all set up for you. Hope it'll be to your liking, but if it isn't, well then you can change it."

"Our cottage?" Aubrey asked.

"You've got to have someplace to stay, don't you? You can't be going back to Earth anytime soon, nosirree."

"Oh." Her body felt heavy in the woven seat of the chair, so heavy that she wasn't sure she had the energy to pick up the sausage slices Richard had placed in front of her. Her stomach won that argument, however. As she chewed the meat (*Even better than that deer sausage I bought at the farmer's market.*) she thought of her home and everything she knew on Earth. It hadn't always seemed ideal, but it was hers. "So, will we ever get to go back?"

Richard had finished slicing and tucked into his share. "I couldn't really tell you what the future holds, missy. There's a lot this old man knows, but the worlds have changed. If you went back right now, and that's provided Driel gave you a lift and she won't, the only thing that would await you would be certain death. Those wizards are tenacious, and they'll be onto you the moment a portal opens."

"But what about the book? I left it on Earth, at home."

Richard waved a slice of cheese dismissively. "Emma will take care of that. She is a librarian after all. Lives for the stuff." The cheese disappeared into his beard.

"But she's ancient!" Aubrey argued. "She couldn't possibly stand a chance against those guys."

"My dear, you underestimate your elders. Emma is capable of far more than you know. Besides, the book isn't as important to the wizards as the dragons are. Nevertheless, it will find its way back into the right hands."

"I had no idea she was involved. And what about you?

You barely said a word when I met you at the carnival. Why didn't you tell me what was going on?"

The old man chuckled. "You really think you would have believed me? If some old codger had told you just how much responsibility he was shoving into your hands, you probably would have run screaming for the hills. Or had me locked up. Then where would we be? I haven't been a Source for the last fifty years by blabbing about it all over the countryside. Besides, I seem to do pretty well on Earth as a crotchety old fart."

Ben cleared his throat. "So where's this cottage that you mentioned? I don't mean to sound rude, but it's been an awfully long day. I think I'm ready for some semblance of stability, even if it's not on Earth."

"Just over the hill and across the creek. Never further nor closer than it needs to be from anything else."

When the dragons escorted them to their cottage, they found that Richard had been quite true to his word. He had, indeed, set up the cottage for them, complete with fresh bed linens and a small pantry stocked with bread, honey, butter, and cheese. There was even a fresh change of clothes laid out on the bed for each of them. While it certainly wasn't the jeans-and-t-shirt type of clothing she was used to, Aubrey scooped up the dress and admired the soft pink fabric. She immediately imagined herself wearing the long dress while she worked in the vegetable garden out behind the cottage, and felt an odd rush of serenity that she hadn't known in quite some time. *Home.*

"Good thing I'm not your typical twenty-first century guy," Ben said as he picked up his tunic and hose. "I can handle this. You okay?"

Aubrey smiled at him. "Yes. I actually, for once, really am okay."

He set his clothes back down and wrapped his arms around her. "Let's go say goodbye to Driel and Hugo so we can get settled in, shall we?"

The dragons were waiting patiently for them outside, Hugo nuzzling his head against his mother's neck for the hundredth time. "Are you satisfied, Wanderer?" Driel asked.

"Oh, certainly. But what do we do now?" Aubrey asked. "The wizards are back on Earth, still."

Driel raised a huge talon and laid it on her shoulder. "You must rest, now. There will be time for planning and training before they make their next move. It's obvious that we can no longer let this impasse between dragons and wizards stand. It will be time to start a war."

ABOUT THE AUTHOR

Ashley O'Melia was born in Denver but has lived most of her life in Southern Illinois. She of course loves to read, but also enjoys various crafts, gardening, hiking, and spending time with her family and pets.

After writing her first story at about 5 years old, Ashley was hooked. She has been greatly influenced by many authors throughout the years, including Robin McKinley, Douglas Adams, Sarah Addison Allen and Madeleine L'Engle.

You can find more information about Ashley at her blog, ashleyomelia.com.

Made in the USA
Columbia, SC
04 May 2021